THE DIGITAL DETECTIVE: FIRST INTERVENTION

By:

Tom Arnold

Illustrations by

Gary Trousdale

Cloud 10 Studios, LLC for young audiences
Las Vegas, NV and Dallas, TX

Summary: A couple of first-year 9th-graders take on a grunge gang at their school only to become entangled with an organized crime family's plot to sell a weapon of mass destruction to international terrorists.

Category: Young Adult Novel

Published by:
Cloud 10 Studios, LLC

ISBN (paperback): 979-8-218-78504-5

Cover design by: Tracey Dispensa

Printed in United States

ABOUT THE AUTHOR

Tom Arnold is an American novelist, cybersecurity professional, digital forensics professor and former CTO (Chief Technology Officer) for technology companies PSC and CyberSource Corp.

Tom leverages his background in information technology and cybersecurity to create fictional stories with real-world examples of cybersecurity incidents. His current book series, The Digital Detective, is written for young adults to share compelling stories with relevant educational opportunities in hacking and digital scams.

Beyond the novels, Tom has been directly involved in investigating and resolving security breach cases involving unauthorized access to computer systems and cloud environments. He has been the lead investigator on large breaches where environments spanned over 7,000 servers and involved complex threat hunting to find the adversary. Tom has provided consulting to the US Secret Service, policy guidance to the US government and regulatory agencies, and is on the steering committee for the Las Vegas branch of the USSS/Cyber Fraud Task Force. He also delivered expert testimony to the US Senate and House of Representatives on the proposed SAFE and Export Administration Acts.

ABOUT THE ILLUSTRATOR

Gary Trousdale is an American animator, film director, screenwriter and storyboard artist. He is best known for directing films such as Disney's *Beauty and the Beast* (1991), *The Hunchback of Notre Dame* (1996), and *Atlantis: The Lost Empire* (2001).

In 2003, Gary moved to DreamWorks Animation where he went on to direct *The Madagascar Penguins in a Christmas Caper* (2005), *Shrek the Halls* (2007), and *Scared Shrekless* (2010) (the latter two being holiday TV specials for ABC), and a 12-minute short featuring Rocky and Bullwinkle (2014).

Currently, Gary is working for Cloud 10 Studios with DreamWorks alumni and founder, Tracey Dispensa. He is directing the upcoming projects: *The Greatest Gift* and *Surviving April*.

Gary continues to write and design stories for TV and feature animation and is now adding book illustrations to his repertoire.

DEDICATIONS

This book is dedicated to my wife and family who stood by and supported me during long hours writing. I must pay special thanks to Colin Clark for his expert research help on Bristol, England and Bristolian; Gary Trousdale for his direction and excellent illustrations; Alexis Scott for her wonderful editing and review of the story; and Brian McKissick a wonderful film and TV producer for his guidance and wisdom. Lastly, there's a plethora of digital forensics and cybersecurity people, especially William Powell, Ryan K., Anton A. Bryce Westlake, and Greg Moody.

AGENT CAPTURED

My name is Jason Palmer. My friends called me JP. My ex-bosses called me Palmer. My enemies just said, "hey you." Or "What the heck was that?"

I'm told I have several problems. You know, crap like alexithymia, an Oedipus complex, and a few other big words. At least that's what was listed on my NSA admission and orientation records that I reviewed after tunneling into the staff records system. The NSA experts always cleared me to work but maintained yellow flags on me. However, the flags may have turned red after my last case where I took matters into my own hands and traveled to Bulgaria so I could verify a lead.

Screw the Washington bureaucrats! That said, I was nabbed by the very gang I stalked into an Internet café game room. As usual, I was right. A tiny redemption in that the gang was led by an old nemesis, Lesta Andropov. I hadn't encountered him in over 15 years. Unlike his kid, Kai-nam, who justified doing nasty things but had a shred of decency, Lesta was bad to the core. Once his henchmen strapped me to a chair, then he wasted no time with idle chit-chat and smashed my face into a table. Blood ran down from my nose over my top lip.

"Take note," Lesta remarked to a henchman. "If they're bleeding, they don't tell lies."

I knew Lesta Andropov years earlier, back when he actually had a few moral rules and a conscience. Now, any vestige of good had long since washed away. A massive Korean, one of his usual thugs, slapped his hand across my face and jaw. Then a direct jab snapped my right collar bone. "What do you want?" I screamed.

Lesta leant forward just inches from my nose, pushing his square, yellow lens glasses up his nose. "Absolutely nothing, Jason Palmer." He stood upright, taking a step back as the Korean goon struck me again.

Goodness knows how long I was strapped to that chair, beaten and shocked. At some point, Lesta stepped back in dressed as always in a perfectly pressed, sleek black suit. He dangled my backpack in front of my face then slid my tablet PC out, holding it between his thumb and index fingers as my pack dropped to the floor.

"Deja vu," he said. "Oops." He dropped it to the floor then ground his heel into the face of the device, splintering glass and bits all over the cement floor. "Fond memories, eh Jason?

Just like our last encounter. What say you? Let's not meet up again." He grinned looking over his yellow tint glasses as he slipped out a white handkerchief and wiped his hands.

The lights went out. I was wide awake but could see nothing in the pitch-black room. A door slapped shut.

Engulfed in darkness, I breathed shallowly listening as best I could to detect if anyone was with me. My hands and legs taped tight to a metal chair; I tried but couldn't rock to see if I could move the chair. The stabbing pain from a couple of cracked ribs and shoulder held me back. My hands numb, legs useless, and crusted blood tickled my face. I sneezed. No Gesundheit. Certainly, no blessing. Just a lot of pain.

I lapsed into a barely conscious state. Two crisp bangs exploded. A commotion outside, screamed commands, and I startled awake. The door crashed open. The lights flipped on. Reba, my oldest friend, stepped in behind two large combat equipped men. She wore urban fatigues, a helmet with goggles and red-laser sight flashed from her handgun. She holstered the weapon. I think I smiled. She grinned as she pulled out a syringe-tipped metal tube that she jammed into my thigh. She whispered in my ear as I drifted to blessed unconsciousness.

After that night, I spent a few weeks in a German hospital, drugged, feeling no pain from beneath bandages and ice packs. My only visitor was a pleasant military dentist who told bad dad jokes as she yanked a cracked molar from my mouth. I laughed. The drugs were so good.

Each day, I'd asked the nurses for Reba, but they had no clue who I was asking for. I never saw or heard from her. On discharge day, a nurse handed me a cell phone. I had a call. My boss placed me on administrative leave, "off-the-grid Palmer!" She threatened that I must stay offline and out of sight. They'd know if I surfaced. In my debriefing I explained why I went to Bulgaria. She remained unimpressed. Even after I provided loads of justification, her deadpan attitude merely told me to enjoy my paid sabbatical, then instructed me to give the cell phone back to the nurse.

Days passed as the physical therapy routine had me walking and moving as though nothing had happened. I was off the drugs but still alone in an isolated ward. Dreams of Reba bursting into the basement haunted me more than the large goon striking me. The words she whispered in my ear moments before she stabbed me with the morphine pen: "You stupid idiot!" repeated over and over. I'd startle awake. Fall back asleep. And start the dream again.

Now that I'm released and kind of back home, I'm holed up in a one room beach cottage off Breakers Point, Grand Cayman. I bought this little escape years ago. A place where I could sit in the sand and see no other human, except the weekly maid. I cherished the white sand beach just steps from the door. My privacy cloaked in jungle vegetation on three sides, and ocean waves rhythmically lapped just outside. Given my luck now, there'd be a hurricane that would wash me and my retreat into oblivion.

Tucked in a narrow ceiling space just above the kitchen plumbing, I'd stashed all my journals and spare equipment. I dare not switch any of the network equipment on, but I fished out my early journals. Lesta Andropov and his horde were still out there and up to who-knows-what sort of evil deeds. They're arms dealers, smugglers, and spies. If only I could've have told Reba what was up. She'd understand. I wished I could talk to her.

I thumbed through my oldest journal. Somehow, it might help me now even though I was only 14 when Reba and I first encountered Lesta Andropov and his dad.

My family moved to the United States after my Dad took an exchange transfer from the Avon and Somerset Constabulary in Bristol, England to the San Jose Police Department detective bureau in California. It was my dad's first time carrying a gun; not just a truncheon and handcuffs. I remember being more worried for him than I was about starting a new school and not knowing anyone. I chuckled thinking about how I used to ask him if he knew which end of the gun the bullet came out. Without fail, he'd flick his big finger on my forehead for the smarty question. It wouldn't leave a mark but really stung.

My step-Mum met Dad while she was in residency at the Bristol Royal Infirmary. She had graduated from Stanford med school, finished her internship, then in my opinion wanted to get as far away as possible from her family, so took a residency in Bristol. I never knew my real Mum. She died in a crash while I was very young. Dad raised me until my 4th year at school when he fell in love with Step-Mum and married. Once I finished secondary school (what would be equivalent to junior high in the States), we relocated to San Jose California. Yay.

The next-door neighbors provided my one and only friend, Rebecca Ng. Reba, as she liked being called, was my age, very athletic, sharp as anything, and pretty, too. For that matter, she was the first girl -- Mum excluded -- that even talked to me. Science and math were fun for her. Athletics, like kicking a ball around, had me looking and feeling like I had two left feet. Reba was a natural, super good at all sports. She planned on trying out for girls' varsity soccer and was already a taekwondo black belt.

Back then, I'd done a bit of programming on a tablet app enhancing an autopilot control for my drones and was testing it out. Little did I know that my technical self-confidence and drive to help my Dad would lead to my becoming The Digital Detective, but at a cost to my new friend.

I'm still haunted by the image of a very large, burly man jumping out and snatching her as we ran to escape after witnessing a weapons deal. He wrapped her in a crushing bear hug as she called for me to run. It's the only time I ever left anyone behind.

THE SNEAKY BURGLAR

It was a glorious, warm early August evening in West San Jose, mid-eighties, dry, clear, calm skies and perfect for a drone test. So far, the modifications to my drone's program performed perfectly. At least much better than the prior day when my drone tumbled crashing into the front lawn from 50 feet up. I selected the elevation to 100 feet now. The drone climbed and held stable, at least according to the gyros monitoring pitch and yaw. I didn't need to look up as the tablet application presented a beautiful view of the area from the camera. Two red colored brackets framed my image, confirming the position lock.

Now, for the big test.

I traced a flight path of a figure eight on the tablet's screen routing the drone 200 yards away on either apex and crossing just above my marked position. The auto pilot worked like a charm guiding the craft around the course.

"Hey, what cha doing?" Reba startled me. She loved sneaking up and making me jump.

"Testing out my drone program," I held the tablet so she could see. "Check it out. See."

"Aren't you afraid you're gonna lose it?"

"Nope. If the drone drops communication or runs low on battery, it will return to its launch point or land in my backyard."

Doink. Doink. The two sounds took Reba by surprise. "Is that bad?"

"Nope," I tapped a couple of buttons near the top of the screen. "A marker's come into my flight range." Reba peered over my shoulder, watching the screen. "Setting drone to seek," I tapped a command.

The drone broke from its figure-8 path and raced over Union Avenue still at a 100-foot elevation. Blue target hairs appeared over a grey sedan. I clicked the target changing them to red bracket symbols flanking the moving car. My drone matched the speed of the motor vehicle as it slipped into a left-turn lane and stopped.

"Hey," Reba said. "Isn't that your Dad's car?"

"Yup."

"Wait!" Reba punched my shoulder. "You put a marker on a cop car?" She punched my shoulder again.

"Hey. Ouch. That hurts. And, yeah, that's my Dad's cop car."

"Do you know how much trouble you could get in for marking a police car? That has to be against the law."

She recoiled to punch again, and I jumped back in the nick of time as her fist only grazed me.

Dad's car whipped into the driveway halting with a screech. The shmoo of a man lifted himself from the Ford Taurus. Waved once at us, then marched into the house. "That can't be good," I remarked.

"He usually says something to us or comes over to share one of his silly dad-jokes," Reba said as I tapped commands recalling the drone to land.

I terminated the flight program and closed the tablet, "Let's see what's up."

Reba scrunched her face, "Should I head home?"

"Naw. We're buds. Come on."

Inside, Dad was standing by the fridge retrieving a Nookie-Broon as he called his favorite beer.

"Hi Mr. Palmer," Reba greeted him with a gentle bow.

"Reba," he said as the cap hissed off the bottle. "What are you kids up to today?"

"Dad, you seem a bit impatient. You usually share a joke or kid around with us when you get home," I said. "What's up?"

He pushed past us and plopped in his favorite chair facing the TV, "Frustrating day, JP. Frustrating day."

"And..?" I prompted.

He sighed, took a swig of his beer, "You know the Pinnacle neighborhood just off Blossom Hill?"

I nodded.

"It's been getting hit right around dinner time every few days like clockwork."

"Hold on," Reba said. "They've got guards with guns, fencing, cameras, the works."

"Yes, they do," Dad said. He downed a half-bottle gulp. "Yet the bad guys find a way in. They case the houses. Select ones that are empty because the residents went to dinner. Strike. Grab jewelry, prescription drugs, and even a few beers, then ditch the place, vanishing like a Houdini. The big brass are screaming for us to catch these guys." Then almost daydreaming, "Sure would be nice if I could break this case open."

"Maybe we can help," I said.

Dad frowned, "Now look. These are not good people. I don't want you guys getting messed up with this. Go play with your drones, kick a football around or whatever kids your age do."

Reba and I looked at each other. I took her hand and led her toward my room. "We're going," I said as he clicked on the TV.

"Whatever," he called back. "Man, even the TV's loaded with crap."

In my room. Full of tech everywhere except the top of my bed.

"What are you thinking?" Reba stepped inside.

"Pinnacle. The neighborhood is a short ride from here. Ten minutes at best. Sunset is at 7:36 this evening. Let's meet up with bikes here at around 6:45. Can you do that?"

"Sure. But your Dad said..."

"Give him no bother. He won't know what hit him when we bust this case open and present it to him."

"Okay," Reba nodded. "I'll tell my parents we're just hanging out. My Dad won't be home for several hours and my Mum is going to some church bake sale with my big sis."

#

At the appointed hour, the two of us rode into a small neighborhood green space just across the street from the fortified wall surrounding Pinnacle. We leaned our bikes against the end of a vacant picnic table. For that matter, the whole park was vacant. I unpacked the first of two drones. The same one I'd been flying earlier that afternoon.

"What now?" Reba asked.

"Here," I passed her my knapsack. "There's another drone in there. Unfold it but keep it plugged into the battery for now. We'll have it ready once the sun sets."

I launched the first drone to climb to 100 feet and hold. Reba asked, "And the plan again?"

"Easy," I traced a route over the perimeter of the Pinnacle neighborhood and began recording from the high-def camera as it flew out of sight and earshot. I looked to Reba, "only about a third of the property line around Pinnacle is potentially exposed for someone to enter. And it's right along this neighborhood border. We'll let this drone make a survey and see if we find anything interesting. The street is pretty calm. You'll help be my eyes and ears."

"Got it."

We didn't have to wait long. A banged-up Ford Fiesta that was once bright blue crept down the street with two occupants in the front. The car went almost all the way to the dead end and parked along the front of two homes that looked like rundown rentals, a total contrast from the neighborhood mansions.

I routed the drone to get a bird's eye view of the Ford. It was clearly suspicious that the occupants remained inside the vehicle after stopping. Dropping to 40 feet behind the rear of the vehicle, I snapped a picture of the car's license plate, then quickly returned the drone to 100 feet and back on the perimeter patrol course.

"They still haven't moved. Should we call someone?"

"Nope. We just watch and observe. For all we know, they're waiting to make some sort of dope deal." I watched my tablet's screen as the drone made another loop around the neighborhood. I stopped near our location with a distant view of the motionless occupants of the Ford. "There's another tablet in my bag," I told Reba. "Pull it out and I'll drop the photos of the car to you."

She was quick, manipulating her fingers and gestures across the tablet. "Got the plate. It's a bit fuzzy and hard to read. Only two occupants in the car." She dashed over to the street looking for the car and then back. "It's about 200 yards away."

"Did they see you?" I asked.

"I'm too quick."

I shook my head. "Come on, Reba. Stay out of sight and be careful."

The light sunk quickly. Soon it would be totally dark. I summoned the first drone to land back on the picnic table.

While waiting, I unplugged the power battery from the second and launched the jet-black drone just as the first came in for a landing.

"What's the black one?" Reba asked.

"I call it the Black Knight. It's equipped with a night vision camera." I navigated it to remain 60 feet above the car. "Let's see what's up there." Reba watched over my shoulder.

The doors of the car opened, and two bright white silhouettes appeared on either side of the vehicle.

"They were waiting for darkness," Reba noted.

The figures met at the front of the car. The two then ran toward the end of the street, jumped a small barrier at the road's end and ducked behind a cinder block wall that ran along an adjoining property. No problem for the Black Knight. It held position as the heat signatures of the two figures walked along a narrow path. They appeared to hop, crouch down, and then disappeared.

"What? Where'd they go?" Reba asked.

"Don't know," I dropped the drone down to about 30 feet above the position. Anymore and they'd surely hear the props. "Nothing."

The heat signature of a cotton tailed bunny appeared hopping along the same position where the guys had disappeared. "Wait a minute." I exclaimed. I sent the drone along a straight course and into the Pinnacle neighborhood. Sure enough, two human figures emerged bent over and then stood. They walked off toward one of the sidewalks. "It's a storm drain. Thank you, Bugs Bunny." I set the drone's altitude back to 50 feet and tagged a marker on one of the figures. The drone would hold altitude above the marked object and keep its camera on that subject. "Reba... in my bag... we need to tag that car. There's a small magnetic box in there. Grab it."

Reba fished out the small box that housed a tracker. "Is this it?"

I nodded, "Yeah. It's active. I set it up before we rode out here. It's paired with both tablets." The figures on my screen turned and went up the side yard of one of the large houses. "Look, they're making their move."

"Where do you want this?"

"There's a hook under the other drone. We can use it to try and place the tag close to the back of their car."

"Screw that," Reba jumped on her bike. "I'll be right back."

"What? Wait. Too Dangerous."

"Back of the gas tank should work, right?" She peddled hard out of the park, jumped the curb and onto the street.

"Dang." I watched the two figures as they climbed through a side window in the house. Moments later, an alarm yelped in the distance. Its screech echoed off the trees and nearby buildings. The two heat signatures reappeared at the same window and ran off along the back of the house, over a fence and through a creek area. They were heading back for the drain that would take them to their car and where Reba was.

The two figures approached the drain. They crouched and disappeared. They'd be through the drain and onto the street in seconds. "Come on, Reba, get out of there," I thought. I flew the drone and held position over the point where the burglars would appear out of the drain. Sure enough, two figures materialized, leapt out of the creek bed, and dashed toward the car. Still, no Reba, but no signs of an encounter with the burglars either.

They jumped into their car and moments later crept past the small park where I stood motionless and alone. They seemed unfazed by the intrusion alarm but maintained a low profile as they drove off.

I imagined Reba face down in some gutter as I quickly recalled the Black Knight. It couldn't land soon enough. I stuffed it and the tablets into my backpack. Where the heck was Reba? Shouldering my pack, I jumped on my bike and peddled hard toward the street and her last position. Just as I was about to exit the park, Reba rode back down the street, jumped the curb and slid her bike sideways before me.

"That was so great," she exclaimed.

"Oh, gawd," I groaned.

She grinned big, "You're concerned, how sweet, JP." She dropped her bike onto its side. "I can take care of myself. So, I planted the tag by the very back of the gas tank. Then, I saw this big, bushy oleander and hid behind it. Great view of the parked car." Held up her phone facing me. "Got this cool vid of them getting in the car with a pillowcase stuffed full of loot."

"Awesome," I said. "But you really gave me a scare. Let's head back and get this to my Dad."

#

As we rode up my driveway, Dad dashed out of the house with his jacket half on and fishing his other arm into the sleeve.

"Dad," I called. "We've got something."

"Not now, lad." He patted me on my head. "Gotta go. Another break in at Pinnacle."

"We know," Reba called just as he got into his car. We watched as he drove off. "Now what?" Reba sighed heavily.

"There are other ways to get the information to him. Come on."

Inside my room, I downloaded the drone's videos, and the one Reba took on her phone. I froze a still frame that showed a blurred image of the Ford Fiesta's plate. After extracting the best possible frame from the video, I fed it through a filtering application removing a layer of fuzz and grain. Next, I opened it using a re-focus application that brought the plate number out just enough to make each letter and number legible. Almost as good as a clean picture, I thought. I added the last piece of data which was the current location of the Ford Focus that Reba tagged. I zipped all of this up along with a quick note for Dad, then with a proud tap of the Enter key and some newfound excitement in Reba's eyes, sent everything to his phone.

Reba and I settled to watch a couple of toons on the telly to pass time until Dad replied. Mum came back late from work carrying a couple bags of Chinese food that smelled really good. "Not as good as the place back in Bristol, but nice," She unwrapped the bags. "Reba may as well stay for some. JP, your Dad's out of luck since he ran off on a case."

Reba and I looked at one another and she winked at me.

At dinner with nearly all the food gone, my phone dinged. Dad sent a message that was only 'WOW'. I checked the tag's position and saw that the car was in East San Jose a block off Story Road. I had the address where the vehicle was parked in the driveway.

The next morning was much like the prior August day. Mum was up early sipping coffee and reading a morning newspaper. Dad shuffled in from the bedroom yawning and disheveled looking like he'd slept hard.

"You'll be glad to hear that we pinched 'em," Dad pecked her cheek.

"That's great honey," Mum said.

"Those videos did the trick," Dad watched me eat a bowl of cereal. "They both confessed, and we got a search warrant for the house." He looked at me. "Call Reba over. We need to have a little chat about this." A few minutes later, Reba came in the front door bouncing along in her usual jovial walk.

"Come with me," He frowned pointing toward my room.

Mum just watched and shook her head as we headed to my room.

"Look," he said shutting the door behind him and staring directly at me. "JP, I know you just want to help with some of my cases. But you both need to understand that there are very bad people in this world. Some of my cases deal with really bad gangs that could seriously hurt you if they thought you were intervening. Last night, we were lucky. Those two burglars confessed, and we closed the case without exposing you."

"We're careful," Reba said.

Dad let off a "Humph".

"And, we're just being good citizens," I added.

Dad flicked my forehead with his finger, "I can't always protect or keep you out of it."

22

THE MISSING MOBILE

Wednesday, two days before the start of fall term, Reba came over with her big sister in tow. Sis was a few years older, a high school junior. I thought of her as the *"popular"* one while Reba got all the brains.

"Hey?" I greeted them at the front door.

"We need to talk," Reba snapped a glare at her sister who shrugged a *What Ever*. "Your room, JP. It's kind of sensitive."

"Yeah, okay. Mum and Dad are at work."

Once inside, Big Sister hopped up with a twist plopping hard on my bed. At least the bed frame didn't give out.

"You've met my sister, CaCee, right?" Reba held a locked stare at her.

"Sure," I said. "What's up?"

"You want to tell him?" hands on hips, Reba held the stare.

"This is your idea, Reebs," sister half sat up resting on her elbows. "It's really embarrassing, and I don't know what this troll can do anyway."

"TROLL?!" Reba pushed forward, but I stood in the way.

"How 'bout you all take it down a couple degrees and tell me what's happened?"

"Her phone was stolen," Reba hissed.

Okay, wow, that's all, I thought. I looked at both of them. "So just report it and have it deactivated."

"See," CaCee sat upright. "I could've told you that's all he'd say."

"You're such a ..." CaCee leapt to her feet, fists clenched, cat-fight eminent.

Again, I stepped between the two and held them apart as best I could. Reba was much stronger than me and could've easily shoved past me but held off.

"JP, it's not that easy," Reba sighed, taking a step back. "There's something on her phone she really, really wants back."

"Okay. Have you tried Find-My?"

"She disabled it."

"I don't want people tracking me," CaCee said. Given the temperature between these two, I was more taken back by CaCee's new conciliatory tone. "I really want to get the phone case back. It has a few very personal things in it and I want them back."

"Just the case?" Reba harped.

"Hey, the pockets have a credit card and a few irreplaceable photos."

I held up my palms to their faces, silencing their meaningless gibber. "Start at the top and tell me what happened."

CaCee told me the story. She'd been out with a couple of school friends at a diner off Hamilton Avenue. They were having sodas and chatting about boys. She claimed she had set her purse with the phone inside it on the floor beside her chair. Three grunge boys, as she labeled them, sat at the next table. Mocking, as adolescent boys do, trying to get the girl's attention. "They're just losers," CaCee said. "Definitely not our type. They didn't even order as I told them to scram or suffer a worse fate. They bailed calling us tramps. Can you believe that?"

Reba rolled her eyes.

"Right after they left," CaCee added. "I found that my purse was opened, and the cell phone missing. Money, makeup, my dangly earrings were all still there."

She and her friends searched the area. No trace of the phone. "Obviously," CaCee said. "One of those rats took it."

"Do you know who they were?" I inquired.

"One of them goes by Wharf. A muscled slug that plays football badly and has a dumb, throaty laugh. A skinny Asian kid who was all grunged-up but with an expensive-looking dang blang hang thang around his neck."

"Dang blang thingy?" Now CaCee's eyes rolled as I asked. Reba shrugged.

"You two are both nerds. Geeze. Get a life," CaCee huffed. "You know, gold rope. A pricy man's necklace."

Ah, I learn new things every day in this country, "And the third kid?"

"I don't know. Never seen him around school. Skinny. Square-rimmed, yellow tinted glasses. Much older. Maybe in his late 20's or more. First time I've seen him. Doesn't go to our school."

"So those are the suspects. What about the phone?"

The phone was an iPhone 13 running iOS 13.3 (behind on updates) and on the AT&T network. It held her music library, videos, and photos. She and her crew used WhatsApp for chats and sometimes iMessage. Since the Apple store told her that she had to have iCloud for backups, she scribbled her iCloud password on a pad of paper along with the phone's unlock passcode. I could have guessed this one: "myiCl0ud" was the password and "1, 3, 7, 9" the passcode.

"Give me a few hours and I'll see what I can find," I motioned toward the door and grinned.

"I'm staying," Reba said her arms thrust on her hips.

"Well, I'm not. I'm so outta here," CaCee pushed past us and out of the room. "Let me know if you find it, nerd-guy." Reba started after her, but I pulled her back by the nape of her polo shirt.

"Not worth it, Reba," I said. "And anyway, I don't buy her silly story. There's something more on that phone."

At the computer, my Elcomsoft tool located CaCee's iCloud account. The password worked and the tool listed out the available backups with the most recent backup just two hours ago. CaCee's phone was alive, well, and online.

I told Reba that the tool would take time to fetch the backup dump file and transport it to my computer even though we had a gig-fiber connection at the house. This all left me hungry, and I needed to get a snack. Reba said she'd watch the progress (just a blue bar creeping across the screen) while I went to the kitchen.

A bit of leftover egg salad complete with shallots and fresh garden cress, two slices of white bread with crust trimmed, and I had the perfect snack. All I needed was a pot of tea and I could have had a right good high tea.

"JP!" Reba called. "I think it's done."

I went carrying my untouched sarnie, but no tea. Sure enough, Elcomsoft displayed that it had successfully downloaded and processed the backup file. The file had been decrypted and exported to create the same type of dump that a local iTunes application might make from a connected phone.

Switching to a viewer tool, I opened the manifest.plist file from the most recent backup. "Easy peasy, this backup was made a couple hours ago," I said. "Know what that means?"

Reba shook her head.

"This phone has been connected to a local WiFi network after it was taken, and I can probably find it."

Once the manifest.plist was processed, I was ready to browse through the data. But before that, I summoned the Autopsy forensic tool to open the files and ingest using the iLEAPP analyzer. Back in the viewer tool, the screen listed all the wonderful content I could search and browse through. I went straight for the WiFi information. The list of connections included GPS coordinates of each wireless access point that were known from Wiggle. Most had map coordinates. Double-clicking the most recent wireless point, the screen popped open a map locking an icon on the location of the wireless access point. This was a coffee shop. The second connection was a game store, but the third appeared to be a residence. Now, a quick bit of Google dorking, and I had not only the coordinates on a map but the street address as well.

"That's just a quarter mile away," Reba said.

"Yup," I tapped more commands. "That's just one vector. I need to validate these findings. But let's see what else we can uncover."

According to the file listing sorted by most recent access time, there were six images created prior to the backup execution. They were photos of a computer game display screen. My viewer tool listed the EXIF data that included GPS coordinates from where the pictures were taken. Two matched the residence of the WiFi connection.

"Perfect, JP," Reba said. "I'll run over and tell CaCee where the phone is."

"Wait!" I typed a few commands. "Let's not be too hasty." Popping open the iLEAPP report from Autopsy, I paged into the video history. The backup dump contained 28 videos. "There's something really bothering me about CaCee's story. The phone's not going anywhere for now. Even with teen boys, I'm a bit struck that they might risk a high-profile snatch of a phone while in a restaurant."

"Alright, so what do you do?"

"I'll fetch an older backup file. One from just before CaCee lost the phone. Let's see if anything changed between the two."

Processing the backup from the morning of the day the phone was snatched seemed to go a bit faster, but the blue bar still crept across the screen. While waiting, I extracted a listing of all photos, videos, and files referenced on the first backup. Once the second dump finished processing, I extracted the same time sequence of files.

"Look," I pointed to the screen. "There's a single video that's been deleted and no longer appears on the latest backup."

"CaCee's not the type to delete anything," Reba leaned close.

I agreed. Carving out the video that I'll call the *missing video*; I saved it on my computer.

"Hmmm," I chewed on my sandwich. "Sure you don't want one?"

Reba shook her head. "This is too cool what you're doing. Keep going."

Opening up one of the SQLite database files, I found the name of the file that existed in the earlier backup and was deleted. "Check the timestamp when it was last accessed."

"That's just an hour after the phone went missing. And look!" Reba said. "The video was created just two days before CaCee lost the phone."

"Now, we play the video."

First impression. This was the exact video I'd expect a high school toots would make.

The video shot along a busy four-lane boulevard focused on two girls nicely dressed. "Come on, snacky babes. Look bang-up," CaCee said shooting the video as the other girls struck poses. The camera then swept to the right focusing on three men. "Hey, it's Kai!" CaCee screamed. "Everyone, say hi to Kai." Then a cacophony of "Hey Kai. Hi Kai. Over here, Kai." A thin guy looked across at the girls and waved. He wore tight black clothes and had a large gold chain around his neck. He was flanked by a taller version of himself dressed in a pressed white suit, yellow-tinted glasses, and a face that didn't look pleased at all. The white suit slipped his glasses down his nose watching over the top and shook his head. The third man was very large and had probably just exited a black limousine that was parked curbside. He held a stubby cane and slapped it on the ground grabbing the attention of the other two. CaCee panned back to the two other girls. They struck sad poses and faked rubbing tears from their eyes. The video ended.

"That kid, Kai," Reba said. "He fit the description CaCee gave of one of the boys at the diner."

"Yes, he did," I commented as I heard the front door slam shut.

"Hey, JP, son," my Dad, the real copper, shouted. "I'm home."

"Now to get the phone back," I grinned at Reba. "Hi Dad, can you come in here?"

"No, no," Reba whacked me on the back. "CaCee can get her own phone back."

"What's up?" Dad poked his head in. "Hi Reba."

"I just wanted to show you how I recovered a bunch of data for CaCee, Reba's big sister."

"Cool," Dad looked proud. "I see you're using the tools that I got you." Turning to Reba. "How'd he do?"

"It was amazing, Mr. Palmer."

"In a few years and steady work at school, he'll make a great forensic examiner. I'm off to shower and wash the crime from my hands. Ciao."

Once I heard his bedroom door shut. "Reba, what gives? He could run over and retrieve the phone from that house."

"Nope." Reba scribbled down the address. "This is all CaCee's problem." She turned to leave.

"Don't say anything about Kai and the video. Let's keep this our secret for now. I'm going to enhance the images and see if there's anything else."

#

I clipped a few still images and zoomed in tight on the three men. They stood by the nose of a long black stretch limousine. A brown leather briefcase sat on the bonnet nearest the big man. Just before the girls started shouting at Kai, the big man held a bag in his hand as though showing it to the other two, then tossed it back in the briefcase. The taller man that looked like Kai wore a pressed white suit with a pale blue shirt and open collar. The big man was all upper-body muscle that wrapped biceps the size of my thighs to the point of stressing the seams. His suit was jet-black that matched the spotless car. I would have thought him a driver until I saw the ornate gold colored knob atop the cane he held. At 30 frames per second, big guy hoisted the cane at the face of the other two, then just as the girls started calling out Kai's name, action stopped, and they all looked across the boulevard. I deduced he was no chauffeur. He clearly didn't need the cane for support. A weapon or tool to quiet adversaries was most likely. Demanding attention from the others, he slapped the cane on the ground just before the video ended. I snapped a close-cropped shot of the cane and the size of his hand covering the entire large gold knob.

Worse yet, CaCee and her chums interrupted something nasty.

X ≠ Y

Friday. Halloween night.

A horn groaned as the motors on the large rollup door spun to life lifting the steel door.

"We're in trouble," Reba whispered as she looked around. We ducked behind a row of crates seeking any place to hide. She worked her way down the row crouched on her hands and feet. At each crate, she tried the lid. One wasn't nailed down and she lifted it. "In here. There's room for us both."

"Wait," I answered. "I need a bit more time to land my drone on top of that I-beam." I'd launched the drone inside the large warehouse to speed up our search but now needed to set it down safely and shut off the whirring engines.

Once done, we jumped into the big wooden shipping crate just as the steel door reached the top and two figures appeared through the opening. Reba was able to position the lid back atop the crate. We were sealed in with only the light from my tablet. Not what I expected to be doing on Halloween night. Reba dressed as a ballerina and me complete with deerstalker cap, coat, and fake pipe to look like Sherlock Holmes. Thinking we could pop into an empty warehouse to rescue a missing pup, suddenly we were the ones needing a rescue.

With my drone atop an I-beam, its camera had an unobstructed view of the door and front third of the warehouse. Outside the door, a worker waved his arms and guided a box truck to back partially into the building. The main lights came on in the warehouse. My tablet screen flashed out all white for a moment until the camera adjusted to the new lighting.

Reba lifted the lid a few inches and peeked out, "They've backed a truck in." She dropped back into the crate letting the lid down softly, "I count three of them. Two workers and a driver."

"Can we sneak past them?"

"Not a chance. The truck's pulled halfway in and is blocking the entrance." Reba scooted next to me as we sat atop thick straw used to protect the crate's contents. I held the tablet, sharing the action on the screen. The men opened the back of the truck then formed a line. They tossed heavy burlap sacks from the truck one at a time until the final man stacked them on the floor.

"I can hear them," Reba whispered.

"They're about 25 feet beyond the right corner of this crate."

A lean man dressed in pressed black slacks and an open collared shirt appeared from a door that probably led to an office area.

"Looks like boss-man just showed up," I said.

Reba scooched closer to me, watching the tablet screen, "He looks like one of the guys in the video you got from CaCee's phone."

I nodded.

The man flicked a knife open and pulled one of the sacks upright that had been piled on the floor. Slashing the sack, he reached in. Coffee beans, or something like that, poured onto the floor but he kept fishing his hand around until he retrieved what looked like a quart-sized plastic bag. Holding the bag up, the contents sparkled in the harsh white light of the warehouse. He squeezed it, flipped it in the air, and caught it in his other hand. After setting the bag down by his feet, he dug again through the contents of the same sack. Clearly, not finding whatever else was in there, he dumped the contents in a heap on the floor, kicked his foot through the piles of beans, and shouted, "Where's the other one?"

The workers froze.

"Well, is there another bag in that truck with these same markings?"

The workers jumped from the truck and then looked through the items they'd unpacked. After going through all of them, they stood still looking at the boss man. He snatched up the sack of shiny objects.

"Those jackals," he said turning to one of the laborers. "You! Get the lift and load those crates." He pointed directly to where Reba and I hid. "Only load the first two of them. They only get half since they stiffed us."

Reba looked at me and whispered, "What was in the shiny bag he found?"

"Can't say, but I guess it's probably valuable."

Exasperated, the man kicked through the pile of beans on the floor, then walked back into the office slamming the door behind him.

"We gotta get out of here," Reba tried to stand, but I pulled her back down into the straw.

"Bad timing."

A forklift rumbled as it gathered the crate where we hid. Connecting to the pallet beneath us, the lid jostled a bit. The forklift stopped.

"Oh, crap," I said as the driver exited the forklift and stood directly over the crate holding a hammer. He pounded a nail into the lid, then walked around and pounded another nail in at the other corner We grabbed onto the side walls of the crate steadying ourselves as the forklift rose us up. I barely held onto my tablet as we plopped down in the back of the truck.

Reba let out a shriek that I muffled with my hand as another crate pushed us deeper into the truck. Silence followed. Then the truck's rollup door slammed down and latched from the outside.

Reba wasted no time positioning herself flat on her back with her feet pressed against the lid of the crate. Something broke beneath the straw as she pressed her feet upward until the lid popped up. We slipped out into the truck bed as we heard the engine roar.

"We're trapped," Reba said.

"At least we're not in that box," I shined my flashlight around the interior of the truck. Aside from the two of us, the crates were the only other items. "Looks like we're trapped in back of a box truck. Probably the same one we saw them unload."

She slapped my back, "Brilliant deduction, Sherlock. Anyone can see we're stuck inside here until they find us when we get to wherever we're going."

The truck's diesel engine revved and fumes leaked inside the storage area.

"This is even better," Reba slapped me again. "Now we're getting gassed."

"Hold on, my drone is still in range," I ignored her. "The work area in the warehouse is clear."

I activated the drone's motors and lifted it off from the support beam. Just as the truck pulled clear of the warehouse door, I guided the drone out and set its elevation to 120-feet up. The drone had a clear view of the truck. I tapped the screen and locked the marker to my tablet computer. The truck gears shifted, and we lurched forward turning onto the boulevard outside the warehouse. Dropping over the curb, Reba and I bounced inside, and I lost my grip on the tablet.

Reba dove down catching the device before it hit the planked flooring. "Please," Reba passed the tablet back. "Try not to lose our only lifeline."

I sat back on the floor of the truck and watched the images from the drone's camera. We sped up on the four-lane boulevard. The truck creaked and rattled and we were tossed a bit. The noise inside the box was the worst. Every movement echoed and banged inside. If we hit a pothole or rock, the box lurched and dropped with a bang.

Reba took my flashlight and went over to the other crate that had pushed ours deeper into the truck. She held on keeping her balance and walked a bit like a bow-legged cowboy, "I wonder what's in this?"

"Probably the same junk that was in ours. Here, this might help," I pulled a small 10-inch crowbar from my backpack.

"You carry a crowbar?"

"Long story. Came with a Christmas gift that was packaged in a small wooden crate. Had to use the little crowbar to rip open the package. Thought it was cool and that it might come in handy someday."

"Today's that day," Reba pried the lid several times along all 4 sides. After grunting and pressing her full weight on the bar, the lid popped off. She tossed the crowbar back to me, then fished through the straw packing and pulled out a big blue-white vase that was actually half her actual height. The painted vase resembled one of the fine jars from China's Ming dynasty.

"Not the cheap trinkets that are in the other crate," she said. The truck curved right accelerating onto a freeway on ramp.

"Hold it up a bit." I stood as Reba hoisted the vase with ease. I snapped a picture.

"Taking a souvenir snap?"

"Hardly," I started a Google image search. "Let's see if we get anything on these."

The truck bumped over another pothole and swung into a right turn jarring the vase from Reba's grip and reducing it to dust on the floor, "Oops." Reba kicked at the dust and plucked out a small data drive that had been concealed in the vase. "This might be the valuable part."

Reba grabbed the small crowbar back and slapped it against a second vase that was still in the crate. After fishing around with both arms, she popped up holding a second flash drive that she tossed to me. I pocketed both drives.

"Aren't you going to examine them?"

"Can't do it here. Tablet doesn't have USB ports."

"Huh?" Reba shook her head. "You carry a crowbar but can't mount a USB drive?"

I looked at her leaning with one hand against the open crate. What a sight, her in a pink ballerina costume on Halloween night, covered in grey dust from head to toe. Her black hair streaked down and pasted to her face. I couldn't help laughing. She just shrugged and waved her fist at me.

#

Wednesday, two days before Halloween.

Reba and I sat in the very back of a full classroom. Linear algebra formulas were penned on the whiteboards along with a somber poster of Al-Khwarizmi, the father of algebra, gazing over the class. Ms. Grundy navigated through the rows of students, passing out graded exam papers that she set face down before each student. She moved silently through her routine.

I stared at the poster and slipped into a daydream. Imagining Al-Khwarizmi kneeling on the ground as he scribbled a binomial formula in the dusty earth before him, he worked rapidly solving the equation. Then, paused and scrawled:

"X ≠ Y".

Reba jabbed me in the side, "Wake up."

Ms. Grundy set the paper down in front of Reba, then set another on my desk. "Very nice job you both," she whispered.

Reba flipped her page over displaying a marked 98%. Not to be outdone, I turned my page over showing a red "97.5%".

"Cool," Reba winked. "We'll ace it next time."

I frowned and shook my head. "I'm sure Ms. Grundy is just leaving us room for improvement, right?"

Ms. Grundy reached two students ahead of us in the second row. The one on the right went by Wharf, and I nicknamed the other next to him as Sluggo. Best I could tell, Sluggo ran a grunge gang that bullied most of the lower classmates, including me.

I detected a smirk as Ms. Grundy set the papers down in front of them both.

Sluggo counted down from three, then both he and Wharf flipped their papers over.

"Bam, baby!" Wharf exclaimed and held up his paper. I could just see a three-digit number on the paper he flashed.

Sluggo reached out giving Wharf a high-five, then said mildly, "Thank you, Ms. Grundy."

She turned and walked to the front of the room. Before she could say anything, the lunch bell sounded.

Heading into the Quad to eat lunch under our usual shady Oak tree. Reba looked at me, "So, what just happened in there?"

I pulled a red apple from my lunch bag and said, "I smell a *Rattus rattus*, specifically *Neotoma albigula*."

"How appropriate. The white-throated wood rat. Very fitting for Sluggo," Reba motioned to the far side of the Quad where Sluggo, Wharf and Kai-nam -- the kid who was in CaCee's deleted video. Kai was not the usual grunge associate that Sluggo and Wharf hung with. Instead of a studded black leather jacket and torn jeans, Kai wore pressed blue slacks rolled up at the ankles, clean white tube socks, polished brown penny-loafers, and an expensive looking pair of designer shades.

"That's Kai-nam with them," I said.

"He's the one my sister has a crush on," Reba looked away catching a glimpse of something in her periphery. "Hey! There's Ms. Grundy." Before I could react, Reba jumped up and ran stopping her. I followed, holding our lunch bags that Reba abandoned.

Reba had clearly said something before my arrival, since the only thing I heard was Ms. Grundy saying, "Keep your noses out of other folks' business." The large woman pushed passed Reba and headed toward the staff parking lot.

"Well?" I looked at Reba.

"She's scared of something," Reba said. "She's way too tough to have reacted that way."

"Like what?"

Reba scrunched her face, "A threat, maybe? Or blackmail?"

I looked out at Grundy who threw her papers into the boot and slammed the lid down. "So, you think Sluggo and Wharf have something on her?"

"Someone does."

"Well," I added. "Seems we have a mystery on our hands." I looked over to where Sluggo and the others stood. "Get your phone out."

I led the way to about 15 feet from where Sluggo and the others stood. As I got a bit closer, I spun and struck a pose while holding up my test paper while prompting Reba to take my picture. She snapped a bunch of photos making it look like she was focused on me but instead captured the faces of the three grunge buddies.

"Hey, nerd-ite!" Sluggo shouted. "Get the hell off and disappear before I smack you."

Reba's eyes widened then frowned, sizing up the grunge goon. I shook my head sharply and led her back to our Oak tree so we could finish lunch.

#

That afternoon I got home just in time to see my Dad dressing for a late-night shift. He clipped his pistol to his belt next to the displayed police badge. "This could be it, Jason my boy," he ruffled his fingers through my hair. "Could be our big break tonight."

"The smuggling case you've been working?"

"Yup. The same. We may pinch the whole gang tonight," Dad slipped the pair of handcuffs under his belt, donned a jacket and headed for the door.

"Is it okay if Reba comes over to study?"

"Sure. See you in the morning," he shut the door in his wake.

Reba popped through the door. "Your Dad's very English," she said. "He just told me to have a super day."

"That's where we came from."

"But you're not so much?" Reba tossed me her mobile phone.

"Step Mum is a Yank and I picked up a lot of Yank terms from her as I grew up."

Reba nodded. I flipped through the photos we took this afternoon, "So what's your plan with these?"

"Watch and learn," I went into my Dad's office and plugged the phone in. After downloading the photos, I launched a search program that he had on his system through the police department. The three images appeared in separate windows on the screen. Blue lines traced over the facial geometry connecting each of the feature points. The markers at the end of each blue line calculated geometric features of Wharf,

Sluggo, and Kai. When finished, a green marker flashed on the corner of each screen.

"This program just calculated the facial geometry of each image. That's cool," Reba said.

"Yup. This will speed up searching across social media sites," a window popped up with a checkbox next to the names of each social media site. I ticked all of them and pressed Go. "The first phase will scan the geometric facial signature against a database that has been populating for the past year against all of the photos in the most common social network sites." I point to a screen that incremented results on the first two images, "The next phase will trawl the internet search engines and may take much longer. It starts with Yandex then moves from there."

"Yandex. The Russians?" Reba asked.

"Yup. The Russians don't alter data about Americans. They publish things like they actually are. Whereas US search engines can be politically influenced to change history. Now, if I was searching about a Russian national, I wouldn't trust the Yandex results at all."

Reba and I headed off to the kitchen and wolfed down a few things that had been set aside for dinner. As we returned to the system, a green bar flashed over the picture of Wharf.

"Looks like we have a hit," I said. "97% confidence and hit on all geometric points. I'm stunned that it's so high."

"Guess that means we found Wharf."

I nodded as I typed on the screen, "It's a game environment called ReconFront."

"Wow. He actually uses a real photo of himself in an online game."

I typed a few more commands into my browser, "Check this. Seems we have his password, too." I fired up ReconFront, a virtual paintball tournament staged in all sorts of exotic locations. A favorite of young kids, but not brutal enough for most teens.

"Let's see what his in-game chat history looks like," chat logs scrolled across the screen. "Looks like he's logged in between 6 and 8 PM for the last several days. There's a bit of chat in the game, but most players use dynamic audio connections within their teams that aren't always converted to text and stored by the game. At least not in this game."

"What should we do? It's almost six."

I had Reba grab my laptop and setup on a table near me in Dad's office. I had her sign into the game with Wharf's username and password. Now we had two sessions running as Wharf. "Nice," I checked out the screens in front of her. "Okay, we can lurk on the game should Wharf and the others log in." I went back to examining past chat records, "Check this out," pointed to a log record, "last Friday, a player named Master and another named Lulimon were chatting with Wharf about the algebra test. Master is touting that he's *fixed* the test."

Reba looked over my shoulder at the chat history. She pointed at a row, "Lulimon says he has more *nibbles* to share next week. What do you think that means?"

"No idea," Only a few minutes before six. "Set that machine you logged in as a non-playing second system. You should find that in the profile. They all support that so players can record game play to post on YouTube. I'm setting my machine to tap the actual game streams."

"Done."

Sure enough, at the top of the hour, Wharf logged into the game arena. Within a minute, Master and Lulimon joined him.

"I've trapped the game stream and have the stream ID," I said. After a few more keystrokes in the game and on Dad's larger system, the sound activated, and we could hear the voices. Sluggo and Wharf were quite identifiable. Sluggo was Master and Wharf was Demon. The third person, Lulimon, had a much higher voice that neither Reba nor I recognized. Not a girl, maybe a younger kid.

We watched and listened to the group in the game arena.

Demon took cover behind a palm tree in a densely jungled environment. Another team's competitor ran past, shooting red balls toward Master. Demon sprang out, shot four blue paint balls, splattering his opponent across the back. Master called out that they should sweep the area leading toward a small town. In route, they shot three other opponents. The status bar showed there was only one more opponent to worry about.

Master signaled Wharf to role left and Lulimon to swing right. They all stopped at the edge of a clearing. From Wharf's point of view, they looked at a thatch-roofed hut at the center of a grassy clearing. The hut had a single door and no visible windows.

"Guys," Wharf asked his fellow players. "Can you see this? Am I clear?"

"Sit tight," Master responded. "Don't approach or reveal yourself yet. Lulimon, run by the front and see if anyone takes a shot or exposes themselves."

Lulimon's avatar dashed by the front of the hut as fast as possible then ducked for cover behind a pile of large rocks. Nothing bad happened. Wharf then ran his character over to the side of the hut and worked his way around, stopping just before the open entrance. Sluggo moved his character to the opposite side of the entrance. Backs to the hut, they all paused.

"Ready?" Master said. "NOW! Hit it."

Wharf jumped out and ran into the hut ready to shoot at anything. "Clear!" Wharf said. "No one here." Master and Lulimon flanked Wharf but a fourth figure crept in behind them. Splat. Splat. Splat. All three shot.

The game reset to the edge of the jungle area.

The avatars of Wharf, Sluggo, and Lulimon appeared. But this time, none of them moved. A new chat session started as the three typed messages within the game. Lulimon said their stream was isolated and should be safe to communicate. I felt chuffed that my tap was so hidden on the stream. Lulilmon's statement was almost a compliment to me.

Lulimon said that there would be "great" stuff coming through and that Lulimon's father needed help moving it. Both Sluggo and Wharf would be paid real well for a few hours' work.

"Drugs?" Reba said having.

"A possibility."

The chat session became heated. Lulimon demanded that he receive payment for what he already gave them. Sluggo responded that he'd come through soon. At that moment, Mum arrived home from the hospital. Reba and I shut the systems down. It wouldn't look good if I was caught using Dad's system in a multiplayer game.

GOBLINS, GHOSTS AND GHOULS

Thursday. One day before goblins, ghosts, and treats.

Dad got home after his all-nighter. I sat down for a bowl of cereal. "How did it go? Success?" I asked.

"A red herring. That's the crap that it was. I thought for sure we'd pinch the big boss," Dad poured a bowl of oat cereal and a splash of milk then sat next to me. "Had the FBI and ATF with us. We hit the place at oh-dark hundred. It was completely cleaned out. Bleached floors. Everything wiped clean. They knew we were coming."

"So, what's next?"

Dad had a mouthful, "Internal investigations now and a lot of finger pointing."

"There must have been something?"

He shook his head, "Not even a chair left in the place. No fingerprints on any surface. Forensics got nothing."

Mum came into the room wearing her white lab coat. "I see it's just cereal this morning," she said.

"Nothing to celebrate here."

She hugged Dad around the shoulders, "I'm off to work. No rest for this doctor."

"You in the clinic seeing patients today?" Dad asked.

"Rounds with the Hospitalist. I'm covering cases in three wards," She turned to me. "You ready to go? I'll drop you off at school."

I was troubled by the case my father was working on and wondered if there was a tie between Kai and the two men that were in the video I recovered from CaCee's phone. I found Reba waiting by the school parking lot and ran over to her. She'd arrived much earlier to stake out the lot and see if she could spot Kai arriving. It was a shot in the dark, but she knew we needed a few more leads. Reba was infatuated by the Korean kid and his link to Sluggo and Wharf.

No sooner had I arrived than a black Lincoln Town Car cruised into the parking lot, stopping in the through-lane. A large Korean driver appeared and held the back door as Kai stepped out. Reba went into an act as though she was taking a selfie but focused on the license plate of the car.

"Got it," she said, showing me the picture.

I typed the plate number into a browser search tool, "Comes back to a Golden Import and Export with a Long Beach address." I typed in more information and found the company's registration, "Interesting."

"What is?" Reba moved next to me.

"The company is registered to another Limited Liability Company out of Denver. And that company is held by a family trust out of Nevada."

After the next class session, Reba and I met up in the hall. We happened to be a few lockers away from our algebra classroom. As though on schedule, Ms. Grundy left the room and headed the opposite way down the hall.

"She must be going to the staff lounge," Reba said.

"We have only a few minutes before the next bell. Come on."

Grundy disappeared down a hall toward the lounge.

"Stay here," I told Reba. "Keep watch." I ducked into the room.

Reba followed me, "What are you doing?"

"Hey! Keep watch out there. Now, skedaddle."

Sure enough, Ms. Grundy's laptop was left logged on and stood by with the presentation for her next session. What luck. I slipped in a USB drive and ran the KAPE tool to extract a triage image of the laptop. The program read the disk and captured the registry, all the log files, and all the user files under Grundy's account. The sparse image had all the important material I'd need in just over three minutes.

My heart sank as I heard Reba with a loud, "Hi, Ms. Grundy."

No time to eject the drive, I just pulled it out once the program finished. Closed the screens and pocketed the drive. As I walked to the door, it opened. I held up my student ID badge, "Sorry, Ms. Grundy. I must have dropped this earlier. Glad I found it."

Ms. Grundy looked at me ready to speak but just shook her head.

In the hall, I patted my pocket, "Got it. I think."

Lunch couldn't come soon enough. We went to our place under the oak tree in the Quad and sat away from others. I opened my laptop. Again, using the KAPE tool, I ran modules to parse the registry and sort through some of the log files. For me, this was the exciting part. "Check this out," I pointed to a registry entry exposed in RegRipper run be KAPE, "There are Run keys set to re-load a program, but the location is not normal."

"Malware?" Reba asked.

"That's what it suggests."

"But why would malware help Sluggo and Wharf? They're not that smart."

"True. I'll follow the malware theory later at home. Might just be something else." I set KAPE to extract a timeline from the files and loaded the email database into a viewer, "This should show us what may have changed or been altered on the system the week prior to the math exam. Could give us a clue."

Sure enough, a set of emails and an image file were added to the system the week prior to the algebra exam. The email message claimed that access to Ms. Grundy's bank account had been obtained, and all funds would be drained if she didn't cooperate.

"Grundy replied telling them to screw off," Reba noted.

"Yeah. And I bet there's a web log entry a bit later where she changed her access credentials."

I scrolled through the list of email messages, Reba pointed at the screen, "What's this?"

I opened it. The message had a photo attached. The text said that her lovely companion had been taken as a further demonstration that they can get to her. "They misspelled companion," I noted.

"Fix the test or dog gets fed to the pigs!" Reba read the last line.

"This is a smoking gun," I opened the image with a forensic viewer that included all the metadata. It's a small fluffy white dog wearing a heart-shaped tag engraved with the name "Trixie". The caged dog was on a smooth cement floor in between rows of shipping crates.

"Could be a warehouse," Reba observed just as the lunch bell rang.

"Let's meet up in the library at two-thirty."

After my last session of the day, I found a table near the back of the library. Since the library was a quiet study area, there were very few students in there. Reba set her books down and sat next to me.

"The metadata tells us this photo was taken by an iPhone. We have the time and date as well as the GPS coordinates," I tapped the coordinates into Google maps. The marker landed on a warehouse building a few blocks east of San Carlos Street.

"That's not too far," Reba said.

"Halloween. We'll be out. Maybe you and I should trick or treat at this place and see if we can find Trixie."

#

Friday. Halloween night. Tricks but no treats!

What a situation. Trapped in the back of a delivery truck along with two wooden crates and ceramic dust all over the place. The truck bounced over curbs and speed bumps while I watched the image from my drone. We had entered the gates of a municipal airport on the south side of the city. I ordered the drone down to an altitude of 80 feet, a bit lower to avoid detection by airport systems. Any higher and winds from planes landing or taking off could knock the drone out of the sky.

As the truck crept between a row of hangers, Reba pressed the lid back onto the crate that held the vases, "JP, we better hide now!"

The truck lurched to a stop, "Couple more secs. I flew the drone down and took a snapshot of the front license plate and watched as the driver and his two associates climbed from the cab. Last thing, I sent the drone back up to 80 feet, holding position above the truck.

We heard two men speaking Spanish as the latch on the backdoor released. "Box, now!" Reba said. I followed her back into our crate, and she positioned the lid atop.

In the darkness, the workers didn't notice the busted pieces of vase scattered on the truck's bed. The forklift tongs slid under the empty crate, removing it from the truck. A minute or so later, a couple of the workers slid our crate closer to the rear door where the forklift picked our crate from the truck. Given the distance the forklift drove, it set our crate somewhere near the rear of the hangar. Outside, the drone camera watched as the three men stood around the back of the truck. One of them lit a cigarette and smoked while the others stood by him.

Reba let out a sigh, "They didn't notice the broken vase."

"At least, not yet," I whispered as I pressed the top of my head against the lid, lifting it enough to get my tablet cam a view of the hangar. A twin-engine King Air sat at the far side of the hangar and our crate was set near a work area with machines and milling tools at the opposite back corner.

"They're still outside," I said.

"Good," impulsive Reba stood up and opened the lid of the crate fully. "Let's get out of this trap."

I tossed Reba my backpack and then jumped to get out of the box. Dumb move as I lost my footing and Reba had to catch me.

"You really need to spend some time in the gym," she shoved me off of her.

Back to the drone. The battery must be getting low. Fortunately, there was a field between the hangers with some utility boxes. I set the drone down behind a large utility box. Switching power off, I caught sight of Reba as the pink and frilly ballerina ducked and rolled beneath a workbench in the machine area. She landed on a perfect three-point stance, knees down and one hand holding her upper body still. She pulled out her cell phone and started dialing.

"What are you doing?" I mouthed the words since two of the workers walked into the hangar and were heading toward the crates. The third called that he was finishing a smoke, and the others should wait.

"Help," Reba whispered into her phone. "I'm in a hangar at Hillview Municipal airport. I see flames and smoke coming from inside." She hung up.

I waved my fist at her and frowned. She just smiled and stuffed the phone under the waistband of her ballet tights. On a shelf near the edge of the workbench, Reba grabbed an abandoned cigarette lighter along with a dirty rag. Igniting the rag, she tossed it into a waste can that was probably half full of garbage. Poof. Flames leaped from the drum and thick black smoke billowed above.

One of the workers yelled "fire" and they all headed toward us. One guy grabbed an extinguisher. Just outside the hangar, sirens ground down as a crash tender hissed to a stop. The tender immediately fired heavy foam that were much like soap suds overflowing a bathtub into the hangar. Fire crews yelled for everyone to evacuate.

Reba waved to me, "Now or never." The two of us dashed from the hangar, staying well hidden by the foam that was already up to our necks. I pulled Reba around toward where the drone had touched down.

"Why did you do that?" I asked after we ducked behind the utility boxes.

"Well, we needed a distraction."

"I'd say that was one heck of a distraction."

The drone had enough power for one more flight. Guiding it up and over the top of the hangar, I got a clear picture of the fire crews and the foamy mess pouring out the hangar's main door. A white helmeted fireman, probably a chief, spoke to the worker that had been standing outside smoking a cigarette. I guided the drone back to land at our location.

After packing it up, I called Dad on his mobile and told him to come get us. We moved away from the utility panels hiding beside a neighboring hangar.

"Dad's not happy," I looked at Reba. Her hair was a mess, and the tutu of her ballerina costume was singed. I was covered in mud and foam bubbles. Thick white foam clung to my deer stalker hat. My hair was pasted down in a gooey mat. My foam coat made me look like a fat guy that had fallen from a laundry tub. Goodness knows where my horn-shaped bubble pipe was. Reba stood back laughing and slapped her knee.

"You look like a fat marshmallow," Reba straightened my hat and brushed off globs of foam from my coat. "With all that, we didn't find Trixie or figure out how they stole the identity data on Ms. Grundy."

I pulled the two USB drives I'd pocketed after from the smashed vases and held them out, "These might tell us more."

We didn't have to wait too long as Dad showed up at the scene in his Ford Taurus with red and blue strobe lights flashing atop the car. The drive home was in silence. I could imagine the steam spurting from under his collar. At home, he marched us both into the garage.

"Mr. Palmer, we were just looking..." Reba started.

Dad swiped his hand silencing her, "No one commits perjury here. Not now." Then he looked directly at me. "Right. JP, you're up."

"Ms. Grundy's dog was 'napped..."

"Grundy? Who's that?"

"Algebra teacher. Look. Her dog was taken and someone's using it for extortion."

"Is that so?" Dad shook his head and growled. "And the dog connects to a fire in a hangar, how?"

I pulled the tablet from my backpack and launched the drone video from the first warehouse. The video ran up to the moment the boss-guy extracted the shiny bag from the sack of coffee beans.

"Freeze that," Dad's demeanor softened. "Do you have any idea who that is?"

Both Reba and I bobbled and shook our heads.

"How did you get from a warehouse off San Carlos Street to a hangar on the south side?"

I continued the video playback.

"One of the crates had a loose lid and we hid inside so they wouldn't catch us," Reba added.

"We didn't think they'd load our crate into the truck," I said as the video scene followed the truck leaving the warehouse. I sped up the playback to the point where the truck stopped in front of the airport hangar.

My Dad paced the floor rubbing his chin and turned back to us, "So, you two break into a warehouse, thinking you're going to find some dog. You hide in a barrel..."

"Crate," Reba corrected. "A wooden crate."

"A crate," Dad frowned. "Then you get loaded into a truck. Taken to the airport. Put in a hangar. Then what?"

Reba and I looked at each other. She bowed down toward my Dad's shoes. "We escaped, sir," Reba said.

"By setting a fire?"

Reba looked up at him. "I didn't think it would burst into flames. I just thought the oily rags would make smoke. We needed a diversion to get away."

Dad rolled his eyes and took a step back leaning against a workbench. "You guys have no idea what or who you're messing with. That guy in the video holding the shiny bag is named Lesta Andropov. He's a real nasty piece of work." He inhaled and let a deep sigh, "JP, send me those videos and anything else you have. Reba, you head home now. I'll be talking to your Pop later."

"Dad," I protested. "You can't snitch her off."

"Jason! Go to your room and get cleaned up. You are oh so grounded and that means no going out or use of tech for at least a month."

#

After a weekend stuck at home, it was Monday back at school. Now I could meet up with Reba even if we were both grounded. We met at our lockers while preparing for the last session before lunch.

Her parents grounded her for a week, admonishing her not to get in fights with other students.

"I guess Dad didn't tell them about the warehouse or the airport," I said.

Reba flashed a smile, "Yeah, I just have to scrub and clean the house after finishing my homework each night. CaCee thinks the whole episode is funny. She teases me constantly. Chirping on about being able to go out while I'm stuck washing the bathroom floor. I may punch her a good one."

"Although she may deserve it," I said. "Don't compound things. Cooler heads always prevail."

"Stop getting prophetic with me," She slammed her locker shut. "I'll catch you at lunch."

"Yeah. Hey, let's meet in the library."

American History class couldn't finish soon enough. Lunch in the library was frowned upon, so we hid behind a few books or my laptop stealing occasional bites.

"Last night, I made bit-wise images of the two USB thumb drives and copied the image files to my laptop," I opened a folder and showed where the two files were stored. Next, I opened up a virtual machine and launched the Autopsy forensic tool within the VM. Instructing Autopsy to load data from raw images, we watched as the tool ingested the data. The evidence tree showed the presence of PDF files, spreadsheets, and a few archives.

I showed Reba the files listed from the two drives, "Now, I'll have Autopsy run modules and see what else we can uncover." She watched as I selected a hash lookup, file type identification and the embedded file extractor.

We ate, acting as though we were reading a couple books but actually watched the changes on my computer screen. Autopsy finished. I opened a PDF from one of the zip archives.

It was a document discussing the quality of African gemstones along with technical reports on diamonds.

"Interesting," I noted. "This PDF was in a zip that had been deleted from the drive."

"Might explain the bag that Lesta fished out of the coffee bean sack," Reba said. "What's in the spreadsheets?"

I tapped open the sheets using Timeline Explorer.

"What's that?" She asked. "You don't use Excel to open spreadsheets?"

"Too risky. Excel talks to Microsoft. This tool prevents macros from running that may also attack the user or send messages to someone".

"There must be over a thousand lines in that sheet," Reba remarked.

"Twelve-hundred and thirty-six to be exact," Each row listed name, address, usernames and passwords. Most of the rows also listed social security numbers and bank account details. "This looks like stolen identity data. I'd say some company got hacked."

"Can you tell who?"

"Not from this data alone," I typed Grundy into the Timeline Explorer search box. "Just a shot in the dark that might somehow tie all this to Trixie."

No results in the first or second sheet, but each was loaded with thousands of consumer identities.

Next, I used Autopsy's keyword search for the same text but across all contents of the two USB drives, "I pulled a full, static physical image of the thumb drives," I boasted proudly showing off to Reba. "This search will cover every bit of the drives."

She yawned and caught herself, "Sorry, I missed what you said."

"Nothing really," my usual luck when trying to act macho. "Looks like we have a hit." I pointed to the keyword search results. The tool uncovered a deleted spreadsheet file living from unallocated space on the drive. Autopsy made it easy to extract into a file into my Grundy Case folder. The opened file listed eight names on the sheet, including Ms. Grundy.

"So, the gang had all her bank information as well?" Reba said.

"Let me search for a few of those other names on the sheet with Grundy." Using the browser on her phone, Reba opened the school directory. "All of the other names are faculty members as well," She pointed at the fifth row of the open spreadsheet.

"I know that name. He's a PE teacher. We need a schedule and roster of the students in classes taught by these teachers."

"Leave it to me," Reba strolled over to the library counter. The librarian was busy down a different aisle. She returned with a large bound stack of printed forms.

"How...?"

"I work here one day a week for extra credit," She waved at the librarian who acknowledged her. "The back section is organized by faculty. Give me the names of the teachers."

I read out the list of each name on the spreadsheet while Reba searched through the roster. It was painstaking work that took almost half the lunch period, but we discovered that Sluggo and Wharf were in a class with each of the teachers on the spreadsheet.

"Me thinks we're finding a gun that might be smoking," Reba said.

I nodded. "There's still a bunch of unanswered questions. Like the source of these files and why the sheet with the Leigh High teachers was deleted and by whom? I don't think we can sound the alarm quite yet. At least not until we find Trixie." I paged through the Autopsy files and noted that the results listed a large number of encrypted files on the first drive. Autopsy identified them as possible digital currency. To double check this, I extracted the first sixteen bytes of each file and pasted the hex values into the Yandex browser. Sure enough, they were DigiCoins.

I popped a calculator on my laptop and typed 12 x 40,000, "Wow. If these are what I think they might be, then the second drive has over four hundred grand worth of DigiCoins."

I slipped the two original USB drives from the table and pocketed them.

"They're going to want those back," Reba said.

The lunch bell rang.

#

Walking toward my next class, I turned a corner, and my heart skipped a beat. Sluggo and Wharf stood at the end of a row of lockers, their backs to me so they could not have seen me hesitate. "Don't look guilty," I told myself. "Just be cool". I started past them holding my head down, watching my feet as I took each step. Nearly past, then a hand grabbed my shirt collar and pulled me back against a set of lockers. Wharf held his paw on my chest so I couldn't move while Sluggo got up in my face.

"Hey, little man." Sluggo's breath smelled of tobacco and eggs. "Got any Halloween candy?"

"Come on, guys," I pushed against Wharf without success.

Wharf spun me so I was chest into the lockers and peeled my backpack from my shoulders. "See what's in there," he hissed. His hand held me at the shoulders pressing harder against the lockers.

"Just school crap in here and this portable computer," Sluggo said as Wharf spun me around. Sluggo held my laptop up high. "Let's see how far this can drop before it breaks."

"Hey! You boys!" Principal Foster shouted in the nick of time.

Sluggo relaxed and slipped the tablet into my backpack as Wharf brushed me off.

"We're onto you," Wharf whispered.

"All of you," Foster commanded. "My office. Now!"

After convincing Mr. Foster that we were all just goofing around, I was a full twenty minutes late for my American history class. Wharf and Sluggo wandered off to goodness knows which class.

Just before two, I strolled out of the school toward my Dad's grey Taurus trying my hardest to act calmly. I avoided the route Reba would take to leave school not wanting to concern her. I was embarrassed and angered by Wharf's departing comment. "What were they referring to being 'on to me'?" My mind raced through scenarios that would have tipped them off. Could there have been surveillance cameras in the hangar? Were there cameras in the warehouse?

"Thanks for the ride, Dad," I climbed into the passenger seat, my knees bumping into the radio and digital controls mounted on the floor. The dull pain made me even madder. I imagined my kicking Sluggo's kneecap and then poking at Wharf's eyes while he held me. In my dream, Sluggo collapsed to the ground while Wharf swung blindly connecting with air as I made my escape.

But that's not how it would have panned out. Reality told me that I'd have been stuffed and locked in a locker had I attempted any such moves. I'd probably still be calling for help.

As we pulled into the driveway, I looked at my Dad, "Do you have a bit of time?"

Inside, I shared with him everything Reba and I witnessed and found over the past couple days.

"You found how many DigiCoins? Twelve?" Dad thought for a moment. "That works out to like... forty-eight thousand bucks."

"You missed a zero. Try four-hundred eighty thousand dollars."

"Oh-Em-Gee. JP, you guys intercepted a payoff. Or, at least, a partial payoff," Dad explained that the value of a bag of diamonds was probably much more than the DigiCoins.

"There's more," I showed Dad the spreadsheets.

He scrolled his finger on my screen, "I see four really prominent names from the community in here. These sheets are the rest of the payoff. Clearly, the sellers wanted the lists and some cash. The DigiCoins would need laundering, but the stolen identities would have immediate value," Dad shook his head. "I shouldn't be asking this, but can you take me to the warehouse?"

I nodded, "Let me pack a few things." I dumped out my books and packed my drone and laptop into my backpack.

Across from the warehouse was a MacDonald's and strip mall. We parked in a row of empty spaces with a view of the building. The main door didn't face the street and was along the backside of the building that we couldn't see.

"Wish we had a better view," Dad said.

"We do," I pulled the drone from my pack, then set it on the ground next to the car. When there were no people around to hear the four propellers, I launched it up to hold 85 feet and observe the main door at the back of the warehouse.

"I shouldn't involve you," Dad said.

"No biggie. We're just doing surveillance, right?"

"I could get in big trouble having you here," He reached for the ignition switch. "Call the drone back."

"Really?" At that moment, a black Lincoln Town Car followed by two trucks stopped just outside the warehouse doors. Lesta Andropov stepped from the car and waved his hands at the workers that jumped from the trucks. The workers rushed into the warehouse and started packing boxes and materials. The forklift began working.

"Crap," Dad exclaimed. "They're takin' a runner." He swore several times, just staring at me, then pulled out his mobile. He called for three patrol units and a Merge unit to respond immediately to the warehouse location. He added that the men were suspects in a federal case.

We watched the drone's camera as the men continued loading boxes, crates, and sacks onto the trucks. Lesta disappeared somewhere. He was either in the car or the office of the warehouse.

Three black and white cruisers swung into the drive at the warehouse and stopped the workers who held their arms in the air. The Town Car raced in reverse and spun a sharp turn toward a rear exit from the industrial park. One of the uniformed officers gave chase on foot, drawing his weapon, but the Town Car jumped a curb onto the street.

"Stay with that car if you can," Dad shouted as he drove the Ford over a curb, lurching into traffic narrowly avoiding being sideswiped. He hit the lights and siren. "Where are they?"

"Left here, then next left," I said jostling my tablet and trying to maintain control of the drone. "They're stuck at a traffic light just around this bend."

Dad radioed we were in pursuit and read his location. As we approached the Town Car, we saw the backup lights come on. The car swerved backwards over a sidewalk, then cut forward around the stopped traffic, bounding onto a cross street.

"I'm going to be in big trouble," Dad said twisting the wheel of the car. "Policy is no pursuits in unmarked cars."

"I've got an idea," I dropped the drone down and activated a scanning function. It picked up a WiFi signal from a vehicle.

Since the signal remained constant as the drone followed, I had a good idea this was the signal from the Town Car, "Stay behind them, but don't chase. Make them think we gave up."

Dad sighed, "Okay. Hope you know what you're doing."

I watched the drone image as the Town Car slowed, "They're a couple blocks ahead, turning north on San Carlos." We followed a block behind them, "Whammo. I'm in."

The car turned left onto a large, four-lane boulevard. My drone followed. We made the light and turned keeping a block or so behind.

"This is great. The car has GM's anti-theft package. I have the serial number."

"This isn't good," Dad stomped on the accelerator. "They're heading for the motorway. We gotta' catch them."

"Dad! Dad!" I pleaded. "Don't chase. I've got this."

He snapped a quick look at me and a harrumph, then flicked on the lights and siren again.

The Town Car jumped another red light whipping sharply from the leftmost lane into a right turn onto the freeway. We followed attempting the same maneuver but were cut off by a large truck. With one wheel on the street and the others on dirt, Dad floored it and passed the truck. Bouncing off the shoulder, our car fishtailed as wheels bit the pavement for better traction. Entering the freeway, we encountered a growing traffic jam.

"Dad," I called. "It worked. The Town Car is stalled out blocking the left two lanes ahead."

Dad slid the unmarked car in behind the Town Car. "Stay here," he jumped out drawing his sidearm. He stopped at the back door of the car and opened it. Then he moved to the driver's door. He ordered the driver out and had a very large man with a flattop haircut wearing a grey suit kneel on the ground with his hands interlocked behind his head. Two Highway Patrol units stopped behind us and the troopers approached joining my Dad.

"Lesta's not in the car," Dad poked his head in the car.

"I'm on it," I guided the drone to fly a wide arc around the area, checking the center dividers and landscape on both sides of the freeway. "Nothing," I looked at Dad. "No sign of anyone on foot in the area."

The troopers cuffed and took the driver into custody. Dad drove me back to the house and left for the warehouse. They'd just got another search warrant and executed it on the place.

Later that evening, Reba was back at the house when Dad showed up carrying a large banker's box under his arm. It was big enough to fit an entire file drawer of paper.

"Hey, Reba. What's more amazing than a talking dog?" Dad asked.

She shook her head looking a bit stunned.

"A spelling bee!" Dad laughed. "Get it?" He set the box on the floor beside the table and popped the lid off. A small fluffy white dog wearing a pink color poked her head out.

"Trixie!" Reba shouted. Reba went over and began petting the dog.

"I just want to say that because of you two, we also discovered a bag of diamonds stuffed in the wheel well of that Town Car along with a bunch of other interesting stuff in the warehouse. Handguns, semi-automatic weapons, and a host of ammunition," he popped a picture on his phone. "Those sacks you saw were bags of green coffee beans from Congo. The Feds suspect conflict diamonds being exchanged for the DigiCoins and data you discovered."

"Conflict diamonds?" Reba asked as she cuddled Trixie.

"Sometimes called blood diamonds," I said. "They're diamonds that are mined when armed factions take over the mines and force the workers into slave labor. The diamonds are sold to support the faction's activity. Gangs like the one Dad broke up buy the diamonds cheap, intermingle them with clean stocks of diamonds, then sell them for a massive profit."

"What an adventure," Mum entered carrying freshly made lemonade for Reba and me. "I'm glad none of you were hurt. Now, Stafford, we talked about you using JP in your cases. He's just a young boy."

Dad smiled, "I've warned both of them several times. But what can I do?"

"I get this was a big break, but you didn't get the leaders of the gang," she ruffled her fingers through my hair. "Promise me. No more sleuthing. And that goes for you too, young lady," she looked at Reba then back to me. "I think a couple weeks with no Internet or drone flying will suffice to remind you of this."

I nodded.

Reba hugged the small dog and said, "I'll keep JP out of trouble, Dr. Palmer."

"Hmmm," Mum frowned. "Better keep yourself out of trouble too."

Dad took a quick bite of pizza and stood. "If it's alright, I'll take JP and Reba to return Trixie."

Mum nodded.

We drove a short distance into a quiet cul-de-sac, stopping at the last house. We got out of the car holding the box. The door opened as we approached the house and Ms. Grundy stood there in a long flowered moomoo and a pair of fluffy sandals.

"I'm Detective Palm..."

Reba pushed around Dad and popped the lid off the box.

"Trixie!" The dog leapt from the box into the arms of her owner. "This is the best thing that could have possibly happened. Where did you find her?"

"It's a long story," Reba started.

Dad waved his hand, "Suffice it to say that we came across your little bundle of joy while in pursuit of an investigation. Rebecca and Jason recognized the animal as being yours."

Still clutching the dog, Ms. Grundy reached out and hugged both Reba and me.

THE SEMPERVIRENS INFUSION

"Come on," Reba whispered as she stepped through the emergency exit protected by a wide-open metal doorway. Almost a month had passed since the hanger fire, the diamond recovery, and the return of Ms. Grundy's pup. Oh, and it was the last time Dad scolded us about getting involved. Now, we're sneaking into some building in the middle of a forest. Great.

"Wait. We don't know what we're walking in on," I said.

"Just keep your cool and let's see what he's doing."

Reba walked to the end of the short hallway and stopped where it intersected with another hall. She peeked around the corner and snapped her head back then held her finger to her lips and pointed toward the hall. I tiptoed to join her as the exit door clicked shut. "He went this way," she glanced again around the corner, then moved to step out, but I grabbed her arm. "What?"

"Look, Reba," I scowled. "Dad made it pretty clear after the Trixie stuff that we need stay out of this sort of thing."

"Grow up, JP. It's Saturday. Nobody's here. I got this." Jerking away, she walked into the other hallway.

I really hoped those weren't the last words that I'd remember as I followed her. This wasn't a good idea. We followed Kai-nam, a fellow student, into a building where goodness knows what happens here. We had only our cell phones. No tech, no backup. Reba just had to notice Kai splitting off from the group after the start of our nature walk at science camp. We blazed a trail through redwood trees, ferns, poison oak, and lord knows what else just to crawl under a chain link fence. Watching Kai fiddle with a power panel then pick a lock, we just had to follow him inside.

The building was spotlessly clean, dust free but the air was heavy and smelled of damp tree moss. I could just imagine my trainers making squeaky sounds on the polished floor and was aghast that I could see every one of mine and Reba's footprints on the surface as I looked back.

Reba moved rapidly and silently like a ninja to the far end of the hall. I followed, trying not to trip over my feet. I looked back, checking if someone followed behind us, then bumped right into Reba. She grimaced, not letting a single tone escape her lips and waved a harsh signal at me that involved only her middle finger. "He's gone into a room. Midway down this passage to the right," she turned back to me. "The room has glass walls that start about 10 feet down. Let's see what's going on." Before I could protest, Reba moved to the edge of the wall, a row of windows started. She pressed her back to the wall. I joined her. I looked back and forth. All I could think of was some person in a suit catching us snooping. Reba took out her cell phone as though taking a selfie, then panned the camera looking through the glass wall. Her thumb flicked on the video record mode.

After panning around the full room, she stopped recording and played the video. "He's on a computer in the middle of what looks like a chem lab," she said. "And he's wearing gloves."

She passed me the phone and I re-played the video. Pausing on a frame, I spread my fingers to zoom in on the workstation. A small device protruded from the side of the keyboard. "Looks like he's plugged in a USB stick."

Reba poked her head around the corner. "Move. Move. Move," she shoved me back the way we came. "He's coming out."

My pulse pounded in my neck as panic set in. We dashed around the corner of the hallway and ran back the route we came, stopping by the hallway that led to the exit. Reba was again, with her back to the wall glancing around the corner while I headed for the exit. She tapped her foot on the floor and motioned for me to join her again. Once more, I stood shoulder to shoulder with her. She smiled at me and grabbed the cell phone back out of my hands. Again, she started recording and angled the three camera lenses to see around the corner. Kai appeared from the passage leading to the lab and stopped in the middle of the hall. He looked down both sides of the hallway, including our direction as though he was waiting for a traffic light to change. After what seemed like an eternity, he turned, walking away from us down the hallway and through a set of double doors.

I breathed a sigh of relief. "Can we get out of here, now?"

Reba shook her head, smiled and tugged on my shirt, pulling me back down to the lab. This time, we went in. There was a wall of refrigerated storage at the far end, lab tables with test tubes, beakers, tubing, and Bunsen burners. No liquids or chemical material were in sight and the burners were all cold. There were two workstations with flat screens on gantries and keyboards. Each station was connected to desktop tower systems. I looked at the one that Kai had been using. It was still logged in and file explorer was still open to a directory of files.

"What is it?" Reba asked.

"Don't know, but it's weird that he left it logged in," I pointed to a folder name. "The base of this folder tree is named with yesterday's date. We might assume that it's the most current," I pulled out my Swiss Army knife. "I don't have any real equipment with me, but I have this," I popped open a small USB drive that was part of the knife and plugged it into the system. It mounted and a new file explorer window opened. Instead of dragging folders one-by-one to the drive, I kicked off a command terminal and ran a KAPE target triage collection. Even on a large system, this should only take a few minutes to finish and collect all sorts of forensic data. KAPE started copying.

"Well, well, well," a voice from the doorway said. It was Lesta Andropov and a strong looking Korean man.

Reba and I stepped back from the workstation and froze as the two entered the lab.

"What have we here?" Lesta glanced at the very same Korean henchman that dad arrested on the freeway. He stood very menacingly rubbing his knuckles and between us and the door.

Reba moved toward the door but was no match for the goon who latched onto her arm and dragged her in front of him.

"That wasn't nice," Lesta grinned like a cat snatching a mouse. He looked around, then walked slowly over to a supply shelf. "How convenient. We have something here," he picked up a couple of cable ties and tossed them to his man. "Tie them together."

Reba kicked at the man digging her heels into his feet and punching at him. No wince. No pain. He just shoved her face first on the ground.

I ran up and grabbed his arm and shirt sleeve. "Get off of her." Next, I knew I was face down on the ground beside her. My hands and arms under his control, he lashed the wire bundler around my right wrist and looped it around Reba's left wrist. Then he dragged us over to one of the benches. Reba was still kicking and executed one high kick while on her back that caught him in the face. Blood gushed from his nose. He pulled his fist back ready to strike hard.

"No!" Lesta ordered. "They are just kids." He stood over us. "You're a feisty one, girl. Tell you what. I'll give you one free pass. Strike again and I won't watch what my friend does to you," he said wearing that stupid grin again.

I looked over at Reba and shook my head to say it's alright. She relaxed. The henchman looped another bundler onto the ones holding us and locked it around the wooden leg of a lab bench. The bundlers cut into my wrist and really hurt. They were very tight, and we were well connected to the bench.

"Let's get to it," Lesta ordered his associate. "Cooler number 4."

The nasty guy with Lesta counted aloud as he passed from the right to left of three glass refrigeration units full of racks of test tubes. They almost looked like soda displays at a convenience store. "Four. Maybe this one," he pointed.

"You know," Lesta shook his head. "We are in America and most things are numbered from left to right." He stepped up to the unit that would be four from the left and opened the door. There had to be 10 shelves in each unit holding rows and rows of vials in racks.

We watched as they carefully slid the racks out, examining the labels. After looking through the last of the racks, Lesta shut the door and looked exasperated at his colleague, "Okay. We'll go through your number four."

The big man went to the display refrigeration unit he had first selected and opened the door. There were fewer items in this unit. "Here." He alerted on a larger rack with three vials of muddy green liquid.

"Good," Lesta slid the tray from the unit. The Korean opened a cooler bag as Lesta set each of the vials in a compartment and then sealed the bag, "Take this out and put it on ice. I'll be right behind you."

The man nodded. The front of his white shirt was bloodied from Reba's kick, and he wiped the back of his arm under his nose as he gave her one final, cold stare and left.

"Be careful," Lesta called behind him.

I imagined he headed down the same route as Kai. Lesta walked over standing just beyond our feet, "Now, what to do with you two?"

For the first time, I was calm enough to notice that Lesta had on powder-blue disposable shoe covers and his hands were covered by blue latex gloves.

"You really hurt my friend, girly," he looked at Reba and the blood splattered on us and around the floor. She kicked her legs at him, but he was just beyond contact. "Cute. Nice try."

Lesta picked up a pair of scissors from a workstation. I held my breath as they were by the keyboard, next to my USB drive protruding from the jack on the keyboard port. Thank goodness, he didn't notice it. I breathed again. He dropped the scissors on the floor a few inches away from as far as our feet could reach. "I'll give you both a fighting chance. Because, in my heart, I'm really a nice guy. Ciao, kiddos," he waved his hand offering a mock-salute then left the lab.

Reba and I looked at one another and then both tugged against the plastic ties binding our hands to the leg of the lab bench. The bench hardly moved. Reba stretched out. The tips of her toes were an inch or so from the scissors. As she stretched, I felt the bundler cut deeper into my wrist. I pulled as hard as I could with her. The bench leg creaked and moved a fraction. Not enough to make any difference. We rested. My wrist throbbed.

"On three," Reba said. "Pull harder." She just shouted three with no count. We pulled again and again. No movement closer. The pain was intense.

"I've almost got it," Reba said. "Pull again."

We tugged and pulled again but nothing moved.

"Wait. Stop. Wait!" I said. "I have an idea."

We rested; our heads sank to the floor.

"It's closer to you than me," I said. "Slip off one of your shoes. Grab it between your legs by the heel and see if you can reach the scissors."

Reba nodded, "This either works or I lose a shoe as well."

She slipped off her right Converse sneaker. I watched as she grabbed the heel of the shoe with both feet and reached for the scissors. The shoe set atop the yellow plastic handles, and she carefully dragged them toward her until she let loose the shoe and slid the scissors toward her free hand. She clipped the wire bundlers binding us to the bench. "Way to go, JP. That worked. Now, let's get out of here."

All I could think of was the thumb drive. I jumped up to the keyboard and started issuing the command to politely unmount the drive.

Reba just pulled the drive out and slapped it into my hands, "No time to play. Let's go." Hopping on one foot, she slipped the shoe back on and opened the door just as we heard a loud click of the lock solenoid. It was noticeably different from any sound as the door had been unlocked when we entered. We both paused, looking at each other. I pointed to a camera as its servomotor swung the housing and red light toward us. Surveillance and locks were back online. "This isn't good," I said as we held hands and ran from the room.

Reba and I ran through the halls back to the emergency exit. She hit the panic release as a horn sounded and the door swung open. We ran hard to the fence line and back to science camp.

#

Luck was somewhat on our side as we ran back through the trees and reached the main camp building just as the other thirty students arrived back from the nature hike.

Unnoticed, we joined the group and went into the cafeteria hall. Dinner was just being set and served.

A student behind me pointed out that my wrist was bleeding and I'd been cut. My first reaction was to pull my shirt sleeve down further, but there was quite a bit of blood. "Must of snagged it somewhere," I explained. "Reba, I'm going to first aid and get this cleaned up."

When I was done, Reba had gone to the girl's dorm. I looked for her in the common area, but she was probably in the shower or something. The USB drive in my pocket burned in my thoughts. I took the Swiss Army knife from my pocket and played with several attachments. I was just happy that I hadn't lost it during the rush to get back to camp. I wondered what information it held from the lab. It could be all sorts of secret things and I really, really wanted to know what was there. I was pleased that the KAPE tool ran so well extracting the information. One of the counselors walked into the room, and I slipped the knife back into my pocket. High school students carrying pocketknives were not permitted at camp.

"Hi," the Counselor said approaching the sofa I was seated on. "Let's see, you're Jason, right?"

I nodded.

"Cool. So, tell me, what did you think about the hike today, Jason?"

"It was good," I hoped he couldn't tell I began to sweat. "I'm not much for hiking and outdoor stuff," I stammered. Don't talk too much, I thought.

He nodded, "That's okay. What was your favorite part of the hike?"

Oh, great. How about watching nasty actors break into a lab in the woods, I thought. "Well, I think learning about how sempervirens defend themselves from fire was most interesting." Oh, I hoped that was a topic they had covered.

"Awesome. They have an amazing defense system, don't they? Kind of built in security."

"The bark grows up to a foot thick and high tannin levels protect the core as well. And they have an ability to self-prune lower branches above the forest floor," I remembered this from a State Park Web site I read before leaving for camp. "Even if they're damaged by a lightning strike, they can survive."

The Counselor grinned, "Good man, at least someone was paying attention during the hike."

Thank goodness he was leaving, then paused turning back to me, "So, what happened to your wrist?"

Crap, he saw the edge of the stretch gauze bandage poking out under my shirt sleeve. "Oh, this," I said. "Just a scratch. I lost my footing a bit."

"Did you see the nurse?"

I nodded.

"Good. We can't be too careful," he turned and walked over to some of the other students.

Ah, relief. I sat back. Now my wrist throbbed a dull pain that was most annoying. I'm such a klutz. As a distraction from the pain, I started making a list of things that I'd do to the drive once I got home. I'd start by extracting a timeline of all the data. This should show me access times on various objects and files. Kai was clearly interacting with that computer. He should have left trace evidence that could lead me to the files he touched or collected. Shy of the timeline, I'd focus on recent activity in the Registry. The Most Recently Used artifacts could give me a better lead. Then I'd look for any signs of malware on the machine. Darn, if I'd only had more time with the system, I could have extracted a memory image. That would really tell me what Kai was up to. Ah well.

I left for the boy's dorm and climbed atop my bunk. A few of the other kids were goofing off and another group played cards at the table. Through dinner service I hadn't noticed that Kai had actually rejoined the class. Now, he played cards and paid no attention to me at all. Not a glance, a smirk, nothing. Just a bool-yah each time he slapped his cards down on the table. They all laughed and would shuffle and deal the next hand.

Nothing could happen to my pocketknife, and I tucked it under my pillow. I and fell back asleep. Startling a few hours later, I woke. I laid totally still listening for any movement near my bunk. I felt for the knife. It was still there. I sighed and relaxed on my back. The room was dark except for the blueish hue of the night lights. The kid below me snored, sawing big redwood logs with each exhale.

Images of what happened the day before raced through my head. My mind played scenario after scenario about what had happened and what could have caused our situation. The alarms and surveillance cameras had clearly been disabled and then reactivated right just as we got free. From the cameras, Reba and I could surely be identified as the only ones in the lab. Thank goodness Reba's composure and athleticism got us out of there, but the camera footage accused only us.

After the whole Halloween and airplane hangar occurrence, Dad made clear that Reba and I should stay out of criminal investigations. Now, we're up to our eyeballs in another case.

Reba disappeared once we got back to camp. She's probably mad at me, and I could have lost my best and only friend. She had to think I was a dumb klutz and couldn't keep us from being seen.

The next morning didn't come soon enough. I dragged myself off the top bunk and dropped to the floor stopping my fall with my hurt wrist.

"Hey, Palmer," Kai stood over me.

I mustered a "hey" as I pulled myself up.

"That's a quick way to get out of bed," he grinned.

"Just lost my balance."

He smiled, "Well, don't be late for breakfast. Every morning must start with a hearty breakfast." He walked off with the group he'd been playing cards with the night before.

Reba was seated at a back table by herself. I took my tray over and sat across from her. She smiled. "How's the wrist?"

"Oh, this?" I held my arm up as I set the metal tray down knocking over the orange juice cup causing it to roll over to her. "Glad that wasn't open."

She pushed it back to me.

"Reba," I leaned across to her and whispered. "I hope you're not mad at me about yesterday."

She looked more shocked than mad. "No. Why would I be mad?"

"I behaved like a dork. I'm so dependent on my technology. I should have double checked whatever Kai did before entering the lab. I really let you down. And, anyway, Kai was back in the dorm last night."

She nodded, "I saw him at dinner. All cleaned up and fresh while the rest of us looked like we'd taken a five-mile walk in the woods."

We ate oatmeal with raisins and brown sugar accompanied by a dense biscuit.

"This is atrocious", Reba said plopping her biscuit on the metal tray. "Did you learn anything more?"

"I don't have any of my systems here," I shook my head, then leaned close again. "Once we get home, I'll do a full work up and figure out what happened."

"I really want to know what was in those vials they took."

I agreed. At that moment, the counselor's voice barked, "Ng and Palmer, your ride is here."

After bussing our trays, we met the counselor at the door, "Rebecca, your parents authorized Mrs. Palmer to take you home." He escorted us to my mum's BMW and opened the passenger door. Reba climbed in the back, and I took shotgun.

As Mum turned onto the mountain road leading from the science camp, she said, "Well, how was science camp?"

I started to answer when Reba chimed in, "It was great. We learned a lot about squishy biology stuff."

"Wow," Mum looked at her in the rearview mirror. "That squishy biology stuff you refer to is what I work with every day."

"I didn't mean any..."

"It's okay. I guess I get it."

"Just that physical sciences and computer sciences are our thing," I added.

Mum nodded, "You need to be well-rounded in all of the sciences."

"It's just," Reba started. "They didn't cover any math or physics related to the forest and ecology. I expected a bit more."

"So, Reba, what are your interests?"

"Math, statistics, and a bit of chem."

Mum swung the car in a right turn and accelerated onto the motorway, "Those fields play important roles in biological science as well."

At that moment, traffic suddenly slowed, and Mum hit the brakes. I lunged forward and put my injured wrist on the dash to help hold me back. She saw the bandage.

"JP," she held her stare on the cars ahead. "What happened to you?"

"I took a slight fall and caught myself on a branch."

"Oh, great," Traffic started moving again. "I'll look at that when we get home and make certain you're okay."

"The camp nurse took care of it," I said.

"Still, the Doctor will have a look and make certain it won't get infected. Are you okay, Reba?" She looked in the mirror.

"I'm fine. He just took a misstep."

The rest of the ride was mostly in silence. Mum pulled the car up on the driveway and Reba got out.

"I'll see you later," I said as she shut the door.

Mum had her entire medical kit laid out on the kitchen table as she unwrapped the bandage. The cut was a jagged laceration less than an inch long, but my wrist was bruised with a friction burn all around. She cleaned and then applied an antibiotic ointment and fresh bandage, "Given what you described that happened, this doesn't look like a wound from a fall caused by a tree branch. It wouldn't bruise around the entire wrist. Care to tell me what really happened?"

My heart sank. I can't lie to her. I looked her straight in the eyes, "I'd taken my backpack off and had the strap wrapped around my wrist while we were walking. I just lost my balance."

She smiled, "Let's see what this looks like in another day or so." Applying more bandages, she wrapped the entire wrist, isolating any joint movement. "Take two of these now," she dropped two red capsules into a cup and passed me a glass of water.

I swallowed them and wondered if she actually bought my story. Reba came in the front door just as I was heading for my room. "Hi, Dr. Palmer," she chirped. "Okay if I study with JP?"

"Sure, Reba," Mum turned toward the kitchen. "I'm thinking of making enchiladas tonight, want to stay for dinner?"

"Sounds yummy, but not tonight. I can only stay for an hour. We're heading out for pho soup."

"Your loss," Mum said disappearing into the kitchen.

We ducked into my bedroom. I immediately educated Reba on the story I'd told Mum in case she was asked. Then, I pulled the pocketknife out and flipped opened the USB drive, "I'll make a image of this drive onto a high-speed SSD, then start analyzing," I explained that I needed to make a working copy of this original drive just to be safe in case one of the tools caused a problem. While my FTK Imager extracted a bit-by-bit copy of the mounted volume from my pocketknife, Reba and I read through assignments from our math and history classes.

The image was ready after just under 20 minutes. Not bad for that tool. Since I'd used KAPE to capture a triage image of the lab system, the files were ready to be parsed. I ran KAPE in module mode building a timeline from the files and data. While this was running, I fired up MFTExplorer and loaded the NTFS master file table from the lab system. Although KAPE ran the MFTECmd parser against this file to build the timeline, MFTExplorer gave me the opportunity to examine all the elements in the MFT file, "The dollar-MFT maintains metadata about the files including two full sets of timelines." I drew Reba's attention to several items whose access time overlapped when Kai was working on the system, "He extracted a total of 6 files. Each of the alternate data streams show that four of them were originally downloaded to the lab system from across a trusted network source, some internal system on the local net. The other two are PDF files and a spreadsheet accessed from the local disk on the lab machine."

"What are they?"

Fortunately, I collected the entire local user folder, containing the spreadsheet and PDF document. The PDF was a lengthy report covering the chemical makeup of subject G.6798.rev6. The document opened with an analysis of three compounds: Redwood seeds, a fungus found on exposed tree roots, and an extract from forest ferns. The next section described a process where a catalyst facilitated combination of the three extracts into an entirely new compound.

"Do you think this is what was in the vials Lesta took?" Reba asked.

I nodded and pointed to the conclusion section. The word NEURO-TOXICITY in red caught my eye. "This is a warning not to render as a gas due to a point-98 toxicity level."

"A nerve gas?" Reba asked.

"Possibly," images of World War I doughboys tucked in trenches as gas flowed across no man's land. This led to a frightening image of the destruction in a densely populated area. "We have to tell someone."

"Who? And how?" Reba frowned. "Remember, we were the only ones in the lab when the cameras came back on. And...," she grabbed my hand just below the injured wrist. "You have documents taken from a lab system. Kind of makes us the key suspects, doesn't it?"

"We need more information before going to Dad or the FBI," I said.

She pulled back and crossed her arms. Although she was way confident confronting danger and had a high degree of tombstone courage, this time she looked really scared.

"I'm scared too. By what happened in the lab, I mean."

"I'm not scared," Reba shook her head as hands moved to hips. "We got caught and just have to be more careful in the future."

"Careful?" it just blurted out of me. "Preparation protects us."

"So..., You have a plan?"

"Let's consider what we know now and what questions we need to answer." I stood by a whiteboard in my room, erased it quickly and grabbed a red pen.

"I'll start," Reba relaxed. "We know Kai-nam is a bad boy."

I scribbled.

"We know he had the ability to disable the lab's alarms and security cams."

"Or someone did," I said.

"Probably Kai," Annoyance crept into her words. "After all, he was the one that extracted the data files from the lab computer."

"Correct. And, he may have had the capability to disable the alarms, pick the lock on the exit door, and disable the cameras."

"My point. Write down one for Reba."

I drew a scorecard on the side and gave her one tick mark.

"When we saw him leave the lab, he probably opened another door to let Lesta and the big Korean in as well," Reba said.

"Wait a sec," I put a tick mark down for myself. "The lab's access control system should have logged the door openings even if the alarms were down."

Reba frowned. "And you know that how?"

"The lab door had a Honeywell access control system. They have battery backups and maintain databases of all doors opening and closing. This will show that doors were opened and closed even if the actual alarm system was offline. Investigators should have at least downloaded those logs."

"You should get half a point for that one. The logs will show the doors opening but not who opened the door. We'd still be on the hook for breaking into the lab."

She's right. Nothing in those logs would clear us or point a finger at either Kai or Lesta. I rubbed the point off the board. "So, next thing," I grinned. "We know from the registry what USB device was plugged in before mine. This has the make, model, and manufacturer's serial number." I held up a finger silencing her, "We also know from the registry which files Kai copied to the drive. And, even when my drive went in, the system records that KAPE, a forensic tool, was used to dump a triage image. It wouldn't make sense to steal documents on one drive and then later plug in a forensic drive to collect image data."

"Put the point back on the board," she grinned. "Oh, we saw them take the vials out of the refrigeration unit."

"Yup, and we know the serial numbers and labels on each vial," I gave us both tick marks. The score was two to one.

"Lastly," I said. "The camera and alarm system should have recorded the time of deactivation and re-activation. This may help our case as well since we are seen in the lab and there's no way to enable those systems from inside that room,"

I gave myself one big tick mark on the board. Two to two. Tied!

We stood for a moment looking at each other and then back to the list on the board. "I guess that's it," she said.

I set the pen down on the tray. "I have an idea. Let's have a look at the other documents Kai copied, if we can. It may take me a bit of time to sift through the cache if they are actually on the system, but I can at least identify them and their metadata. While I'm doing that, you use that other computer and search for Kai's physical address." The drive containing the triage data we collected from Ms. Grundy's computer was still on the desk. I tossed it to her, "There's probably not much in the public domain about where he lives, but you might find student registration files under the C-Users folder on Grundy's system. This assumes Kai is in a math class. Grundy should have class rosters in there that may have home addresses."

We worked with only the sound of keyboard clicks breaking the silence. My tools took time to parse the data and search directories, but I collected a lot about the other files.

"Got it!" Reba said. "Check this out. His address is about six blocks away in the Pinnacle neighborhood."

"The same area where we caught the burglars?"

"One in the same," Reba said pumping her fist above her head. "And, even better, guess who is listed as his parent?"

I shrugged.

"Lesta Andropov."

"Double WAM!" I jumped up and gave Reba two check marks on the board, then wrote in the information. I also wrote the names of all the files Kai had copied to his thumb drive as well as the make and model of the drive itself.

"What's our next move?"

I pointed to the dresser where my two drones rested. "Time for a bit more field surveillance," I said. Then opening the top drawer, I took out a small WRT device that had two network ports. "And, if we get a chance, we might just install this network tap as well."

PROBING RAID

That evening after dinner, Dad and Mum conveniently fell asleep on the sofa watching a British sitcom. Mum curled in his arms and Dad snored away. Earlier, they said I could head over to Reba's to try out a new video game on her console as long as I was home by ten. Instead of gaming, we grabbed our bikes and met in front of my house.

Just after 6 PM on a nice, cool California evening with the sun setting behind the western hills, we rode carefully in the dusk past the main entrance to the Pinnacle neighborhood. Three security guards manned the entrance. Their patrol vehicle was parked facing the main gate. Since the sneaky burglars were caught -- thanks to Reba and me, I kind of hoped that Pinnacle's security staff had returned to a more normal routine of protecting the front gate and cruising around in their patrol car.

Ending up in the same park and picnic table where we'd headquartered our catch of the sneaky burglars, Reba leaned her bike against the table and helped me extract the black knight drone from my bag. Darkness had set in, and the air became crisp. Most families were preparing for the Thanksgiving holiday, while we had other plans. I launched the drone to fly a patrol route over the neighborhood angling the night-vision camera down for a clear view. Although the splash of light from the street lamps gave an eerie, almost surreal appearance on the screen, the images were quite clear. As I expected on this quiet evening, not much moved around in the streets. The heat signature of a couple walking a nearby loop road with a dog on a leash was the only significant movement. The poor animal would lag behind until the leash was taut forcing the couple to tug until the dog had no choice but to comply.

Kai's home was on the far southwest corner of the neighborhood. It sat on the middle of a large pie-shaped lot at the end of a cul-de-sac surrounded by a bunch of bright landscape lights. The lot looked to be about two and a half acres. I paused the black knight's patrol route and flew manually over portions of the lot that faced the street. The house was mostly dark. Nothing moved around the street in front, so I brought the drone down to have a look at the entrance. Fronting the street was a large stone wall interrupted only by a tall gate. I flew a bit closer to the gate dipping the drone down briefly to snap an image illuminated only by the spray of light from two streetlamps. Then I flew the drone up to 80-foot elevation and held position over the gated entrance.

"What was that on the gates?" Reba asked, her breath condensing in the cold and nearly fogging my tablet's screen.

"Let's have a look at the recording in a second session," I restarted the drone's camera recording to a new file and then opened the saved the prior video to a file share. The drone would hold position and wait for my next command, in the meantime, I played back the earlier recording and froze on the best image of the front gate. The dark silhouette of a large dragon with the head of a horse and a sphere-shaped object in its right claw glared down upon anyone who passed close by on the street.

"Whoa," I said. "That gate must have cost a fortune."

The dragon had four legs, a long snake-like body, the horned face of a stag, a wide head with gaping jaws, the neck of a serpent, claws of an eagle, and large pointed ears.

"It's one of the nine Chinese dragons! See the ball in its grasp?" Reba pointed to the sphere clutched in its claws. "That's classic."

"No wings," I noted.

"They fly and travel using magic. But mostly, they're each in control of an earth element."

"Okay, so which element is this one in control of?"

"Can't tell from this image."

At that moment, a long dark car approached the gates from the house and stopped, waiting for the gates to open. I flipped back to the live drone image on the screen.

"Can you see who's in the car?" Reba asked.

"It's a big sedan. In the dark, I can't even see the occupants," I directed the drone to fly a bit lower but stopped at about 30 feet up. "I don't dare take the drone further."

"That looks like the car I saw taking Kai to school and the same one that was in the video CaCee captured," Reba observed. "At school, it was driven by the same goon I kicked in the face, probably has a broken nose and a couple of black eyes courtesy of me."

Always ready to claim credit for her physical prowess, I just nodded, then reduced the screen size to have map control and traced my fingers over the area where the house was situated. "Let's see if I can tell if anyone is inside and where they might be."

We watched as the drone swung in and captured images of the first and second floor rooms, capturing the front, side and back of the house. My survey was based entirely on whether or not lighting changed in the rooms or heat signatures materialized. With many homes, the black knight's camera could penetrate glass windows capturing heat signatures inside. But low-E coatings or security tints prevented most human heat signatures from leaking out. Two windows were illuminated on the second floor by the back, southwest corner of the house and a very large human figure stood on a balcony. An occasional bright flare of light at the figure's head appeared. Must be smoking something like a cigar.

I flew the drone in ever-expanding circles around the residence gently gaining altitude with each pass. Once the drone had a full view of the property, I held a viewing position from the back of the property. The house consisted of two wings connected in an L-shape. In the back yard, there was a large pool and gardens with what looked like a gazebo at the back of the property. At the corner of the house, a small heat signature appeared as though leaping from the top of the perimeter fence and landing on its feet. The drone held position as I used the camera's zoom function to get a tighter look, "It's a cat."

Reba reached in and stretched her fingers even more across the camera image focusing on the animal. "Looks like a fat cat," she said. The animal strolled toward the back side of the house. Each step was placed carefully and silently and then disappeared. "Where'd it go?" Reba asked.

We looked at one another. At the very same time, we must have had the exact same thought.

"A pet door," we said at the same time.

"Good chance there's no motion alarm inside the house then," I added. "A point of entry!" I maneuvered the black knight to hold station above the front gate of the property. We had our eye-in-the-sky now in case the car came back.

We packed up my tablet and jumped back on our bikes. Reba led as we headed for the drainage ditch that the sneaky burglars used to breach the Pinnacle neighborhood. At the end of the street, there was just a simple wooden barrier that blocked any further access. We jumped the barrier and planted our bikes in a place where they couldn't be seen by any car's headlights passing by. It was very dark, and I stumbled once following Reba's steps. She turned and caught me.

"It's too dark. Too many obstacles."

"Come on, just hold my hand and I'll guide you." Reba slapped my shoulder then grabbed my hand. Not a reassuring pat. More like a scolding followed by a yank toward the ditch. "We may not get a better chance."

The drainpipe was not the kind of place I'd willingly climb into. Reba pulled me around in front of her then pointed to the gaping darkness of the drain's mouth. It was rough cement, about four feet in diameter. Dry as a matchstick since we hadn't had much rain yet. We hunched over. My shouldered backpack wouldn't fit, so Reba helped pull it off. I had to carry this ahead of me into a black hole. At least any snakes might strike it before me, I thought. Reba followed occasionally pushing both hands against my butt if I didn't move fast enough. Our backs pressed against the top, sliding with each step. Oh, and it was dirty! Total filth! Rabbits, snakes, and burglars were the only ones that used this thing now.

We emerged and stood. It only took us a few minutes to get through. I stretched. "Wait. Stand very still," Reba said. She brushed her hand rapidly across my back.

"What was it?" I whispered harshly.

"You know that scene at the start of Indiana Jones's first movie?"

"Yesss," I froze in place.

"Well, it wasn't that," she slapped my shoulder. "Now let's go before we're caught."

"That was just plain evil," I followed her up to the sidewalk along the perimeter road. "The house is at the end of this road to the right."

She peeled off her dark hoodie and stuffed it in her small pack. I did the same. I wore a smart collared shirt, and Reba a deep blue blouse and black slacks. We looked the part of rich kids out for a stroll except it was freezing cold.

LED streetlamps illuminated our path as we walked at a firm pace, not a run, not a jog, but not a lollygag. Each home we passed fronted acre lots, except for the compound we headed toward which was secured by a 7-foot stone wall interrupted only by a large wrought iron dragon gate. It was even more ornate than what we saw as the drone's camera image. The two gates rose at least 12 feet flanked by thick walls enclosing the full lot where the house stood. The snake-like body's massive head greeted all who approached with a fanged grin.

I grabbed Reba's arm, stopping her just before she crossed in front of the gates, "cameras."

She stepped back.

Pulling my tablet PC from my bag, I summoned the black knight to fly along the perimeter of the property and return to station over the gate. The image showed two human heat signatures generated by Reba and me by the side of the gated entrance. I brought the drone down a bit and flew a pattern in front of the house.

The night vision camera was pretty good even though it wasn't military grade. Behind the gates, a single drive led to a large asphalt loop. I could see an area of four double-wide garage doors and what looked like a row of second-story windows above the garage. An enclosed passage connected the garage to the main house. I ordered the drone around to the back of the house by the garden and pool. I was pleased to see that there had been no changes in the lights shown from the house since we first arrived. The large figure that had been smoking on the upper balcony at the back was no longer in sight.

"What now?" Reba asked.

I looked at her, "let me check the perimeter once more." I traced my finger on a route that would get the drone along the edge of the property from the place where we stood to the very back corner. The wall only covered three sides of the property. The front, where we were stood, and the two sides adjoining neighbor properties. The rear was probably some other type of fence that adjoined an open space area.

"See any cameras?"

I shook my head, "nothing." I pointed to the gates. "There are two static cameras just inside the gates and a dome camera that's probably a high-def, pan-tilt-zoom we'd better avoid. There's a hedge row just a foot or so behind the front wall along here." I pointed from the side of the gate where we stood down to the corner of the property line, about 30 feet away.

"So, we go over the wall there, right?" Reba jumped up latching her hands on the top of the wall and pulled herself up with a perfect crab-crawl, then disappeared.

I set the Black Knight on a course that would guide it along the backyard to the front gate and back again. The drone left on the route as I packed the tablet into my backpack. I have no clue what Reba thought I'd do next. The wall was a formidable obstacle. I looked around for a bit. Nobody was around. Still, I thought about what I might say if challenged since I was a high school teen just standing by a rich guy's house, in a neighborhood where homes were burgled. At that moment, a garden hose flopped over the wall, and I could just hear Reba's harsh whisper, "grab it and use your legs."

Okay. I grabbed on and pressed my legs into the wall as Reba commanded. She pulled from her end, and I made slow work rising up the wall. Reaching the top, I flattened my chest against the craggy stones, then kicked my legs to lay chest down atop the wall.

"Jump," Reba said. "It's only a few feet."

I shook my head, envisioning my ankle twisting in pain.

"Come on," She waved. "You got this. Now jump."

Sliding my legs carefully around, I really didn't want to jump. Instead, I carefully got into position, hanging by my arms. Reba didn't need to say a thing as I could sense her exasperation. Once my arms were fully outstretched, I let go and dropped the remaining few feet.

"Good grief," Reba said catching me. We moved to the edge of the hedge row and looked around at the house.

"Let's work our way down the side of the house to where the cat went inside." The outside landscape lighting lit up everything except the hedge we were behind. Hugging the wall and shadows, we tiptoed quickly around to the back of the house and the far wing. We came to the backyard. There was a large lap-pool at the center and a covered outdoor kitchen. Pausing, we looked carefully through the yard. Nothing moved. Reba pointed out a door near where the two wings adjoined.

"I see a way," Reba started to, but I grabbed her and pulled her back.

"No. Look up there," the silhouette of a very large man stepped back out onto the upper balcony along the far wing. He lit a stubby cigar. We froze. He was huge with very broad shoulders and a sculpted face that were illuminated as he flicked his gas lighter. He puffed hard billowing a plume of smoke that floated across the entire balcony. After a moment, he sat back in a deck chair and kicked his feet up onto the balcony rail.

"Great," Reba glanced at me. "What now?"

At that moment, the man set his burning cigar down as his cell phone rang. "Where are you guys?" he bellowed, picking up his cigar and sucking in a large drag. "Were the boys there?"

A pause as the caller must be answering. "Don't give me that crap. Were they there or not?"

"He's looking away," I whispered. "Go."

"And," the big man's voice bellowed another command.

We ran toward the back door. Sure enough, there was an animal door in the wall set next to a normal door. We pressed our backs into the wall, and I peeked toward the balcony. Still on the phone and puffing his cigar once again.

Reba reached for the doorknob, but I stopped her, "No, a lot of alarms have a door chime. We go in with the pets."

She slid through with ease. I passed my pack in and just squeezed through. Inside, we stood in a laundry room with four large machines, a folding table and ironing board.

It's really too bad I couldn't do a complete survey of the house in daylight since I might see where utilities like cable TV connect into the house. This would give me a clue about where the data headend might be located. For now, we'd just need to search. Reba started for the interior door, but once again, I pulled little Miss Enthusiasm back. I retrieved a couple of blue hospital shoe covers out of my backpack and handed her a pair. "Slip these over your shoes," I put on a pair myself. "This house is probably kept immaculate, and they might see our footprints or dirt on the floors."

She nodded as I handed her a pair of blue medical gloves as well. "How nice," Reba said snapping them on. "They match the boot covers... We're matchie matchie."

Good grief, I can't believe her, "Be serious."

She punched me hard on the shoulder, "I'm more serious than you think."

I twisted the doorknob and pulled the laundry door open hoping it wouldn't squeak. It didn't, but the cat did! Seeing the open door, the orange and white tabby leapt down from atop one of the washers and dashed into the house.

"Wait!" Reba bent down snapping her fingers. "Here kitty, kitty."

"Bloody cat," I said. "Let's hope it stays downstairs. "Come on. And go slow." I didn't want her usual highspeed self to go trotting off and getting us in bigger trouble.

Polished hardwood floors lined the hallway. Side tables were more of a stand for very expensive art. "This way," I pointed down the leftmost wing hallway. Behind us was a spiral staircase that led from the entry chamber and doors that probably led to the garages.

"This place is huge," Reba commented. "How are we supposed to find it without searching every closet?"

I held up my fist just like the military guys did on TV. We stopped almost at the end of the hall. I pulled my tablet out activating a network search tool that graphically illustrated wireless access point signal strengths. There were several access points in the house but one was stronger than the others. "Assuming some of the wireless access points aren't wired and connected using WDS, I'm hoping one of these is the master and near the headend. Look here," I pointed to the third device listed. "This one doesn't use wireless distribution to synchronize the devices. It's wired and probably located on this floor. If we find it, we may find the headend."

I stepped around Reba using my tablet like a divining rod as I shuffled down the hall. The signal levels of the various access points lowered, but the wired one got much stronger as I moved. She watched close behind me.

"This way," I motioned for her to follow as I went to the last door in the hall. The twin glass doors stood open to a darkened room and we entered a very large office. "That looks like a closet." I motioned toward a door by the wall. "Check in there," I said to Reba while I went around the desk. The signal strength dropped a tad. She opened the door. This was no closet. It was a room built as a commercial grade data center with two racks filled with machines.

"Lots of flashing green lights in here," Reba observed.

As we stepped in, I shut the door behind us. "Easy now," I held my finger to my mouth. "Don't need a single sound right now." I flicked on a tiny flashlight and scanned the room. I couldn't see any cameras. That didn't mean there weren't cameras or microphones inside the machine racks. We examined each rack carefully and just looked through the front grates of the racks. The cabling inside was a complete rat's nest of a mess. Immaculate house and crappy install of the system. They couldn't dress the cables and it hung like some nest of wires in tree. This would make the long-term survival of what I needed to do much higher.

"Bingo," At the top of one of the racks was a Cisco 505 firewall/router device. A single cable modem sat on a shelf beneath a red Cat-6 cable connecting the two. A yellow Cat-6 cable ran from the 505 to a 24-port switch bank. Nearly all of the 24 ports were occupied by blue, green, black, and yellow cables. Again, another mess. "Okay, this is what I need," I said. "Reba, do you see the blue-green color of this Cisco firewall device?"

"Yeah."

"Look through the other racks and see if there's any other box like this labeled 'VPN Concentrator'."

Reba took a second flashlight and looked at the other machines mounted below and in the two other racks. "Nothing," she whispered.

"Excellent," I dug out a small black box that was just 4 by 4 square and about an inch thick. It had two Ethernet ports and a power port.

"What's that?" Reba asked as I slid out a small plastic bag that contained a bunch of decals.

"It's a tap," I slid a Cox Communication company decal and logo out of the plastic bag and stuck it carefully to the front of my box. "Now it will look a bit more official in case someone finds it." Flipping it over, I stuck another decal identifying the box as a performance enhancer and listing a toll-free phone number to call if someone had questions or needed help.

"Whose toll-free number is that?" Reba asked.

"If someone calls, one of my cloud machines will answer, and I'll have time to respond."

"Wow, you think of everything."

I smiled, "Now, go out and watch the hallway. Signal me if anything goes weird or you see that dumb cat going up the stairs."

Reba rolled her eyes as though she didn't quite trust me and left the closet for a position just inside the office doors.

Once she was there, I gave her a quick thumbs up. She peeked around the corner down the hall and returned my thumbs up.

I unplugged the wire connecting the firewall to the switch and connected it to one of the ports on my device then connected a cable from my device back to the firewall. I held my breath. No alarms. No signals. And no sign from Reba. All should be good. I plugged my device into a power strip then cautiously buried my device behind the mass of dangling Ethernet cables. Done. I shut the data rack and closet, gently pushing the closet door shut before joining Reba.

"Let's make like sheep," I said pushing past her and out of the office. "And get the flock out of here."

We were almost back to the laundry room when a loud sneeze echoed from upstairs. "Who let the cat out?" The big man's voice barked followed by another sneeze.

Panic! We held our backs to the wall listening for any sounds of movement. Another sneeze and rattling nose blow.

Reba mouthed the words, "The cat."

Wide-eyed clown grin from me.

The electric motors of the garage door activated. Reba and I slid along the wall back into the laundry room pulling the door closed behind us.

We paused, holding our breath as the booming voice yelled. "Kai! Lesta! You let the cat out again."

"It's us, papa. We're back." Lesta said.

"Get your butts up here and catch this cat."

Footsteps clamored up the staircase.

We stood in silence. I breathed again.

"Now's our chance." Reba had slipped the shoe covers and socks off and dove toward the cat door.

I took a step forward directly into the litter box and water bowl. No time. I shoved my pack through and followed her holding the smelly shoe covers in my fingertips.

Once outside, we stood against the wall for a moment.

"Pee ewe. What is that smell?"

I dangled out the soiled shoe cover still in my gloved hands. I started to stuff them in my pack when Reba grabbed me.

"You really are a klutz," she grabbed my forearm and the top of my gloved hand holding the covers, then peeled the glove off my hand and over the cover concealing it inside. I pulled the other one off and stuck both in my pack. "As soon as we find a can somewhere, ditch those things!"

Up in the window where the big man had stood smoking, we could just see the thin frames of Lesta and Kai facing the giant man. Gestures gave us a clue they were in a heated conversation, and Kai ran from the room chasing something, probably the cat.

"Now. Let's move." Reba nudged me. Not the usual punch or slap on the back. I'm making progress with her.

We followed our path back around to the front of the house wall to where we dropped in. "What now? The hose again?" I asked.

She frowned. "No, dummy. This time you go first." Reba interlocked her hands and crouched a bit. She boosted me up until I was able to grab the top of the wall and squirm the rest of the way on my own to lay flat on the top.

Nothing moved outside on the street. Reba jumped as she did before, grabbed the wall top and crab-walked scaling up. She swung her body over and dropped to a crouch that Natasha Romanov would be proud of. I can't do that. I held tight to the top of the wall glancing occasionally down at Reba. She waved for me to follow. As before, I slowly drifted over hanging with my arms fully outstretched, then let go.

"You really need to work out more," Reba said as we headed off down the street. Aside from a lot of dirt and dust on our clothes, we looked pretty presentable, I mused.

It was my turn to pull Reba in between the wall and a broad green shrub. Reba was about to speak, but I held my finger up silencing her as I pulled out my tablet.

I had just enough signal from the tap's own wireless signal to connect. My tap was actually a wireless WRT unit that I'd flashed with Yocto Linux. It worked like a charm. I was in with a root shell. The tap was intercepting network traffic as we watched a packet counter climb. But this wasn't the important thing right now. Persistence and stealth were the main factors.

Kai was a smarty with computers considering what he pulled off at the redwood lab. Bypassing alarms, deactivating electronic doors, and killing the CCTV feed was no small feat. So, I knew it would be easy for him to detect my tap as soon as he saw a rogue wireless access radio broadcasting in his home. After all, the radio on my tap may have already set off alarms so I needed to kill that real soon.

My objective was simple. In the next few taps, I commanded a discover script to grab both the internal and external IP addresses for the network. This happened in a blink. The next command kicked off a reverse shell connecting the tap to an open Netcat port on one of my cloud servers. This would let me remotely log into the tap without anyone noticing. Then, another reverse shell to a port on a separate cloud server as a backup; just in case the first shell failed. Done. Now, I killed the tap's radio frequency transmitter and took a deep breath. The tap was hidden from easy detection, and I could relax. Unless Kai ARP-scanned his own network, which was doubtful, he shouldn't find it.

"Hurry up," Reba said.

"Almost done. The tap just discovered both internal and external IP addresses. I have direct control from anywhere." I looked at her with a clown grin again, "We're good." I logged out and shut down my tablet, which I stuffed back in my pack.

"What if it loses the connection?" We stepped out onto the empty sidewalk.

"Not an issue. If the connection drops, it will reconnect at random intervals. Just like a bad guy's malware but better. It's physical."

Reba paused and thought for a moment then frowned at me, "Are we the bad guys now?"

"No," I snapped. "We're the good guys just collecting evidence on some nasty bad actors. Now, let's bugger off."

She brought up a good point that made me think. Sometimes there's a very fine line between hacking and detecting for justice.

While we headed out of Pinnacle, I knew the tap was kicking off several more automated actions. The first function launched a simple, dynamic request through port 443 across three Web sites. Each site reflected the tap's external network details. This was an important part of discovery since we didn't know the IP addresses assigned to Kai's network and how the firewall was configured to perform address translation. The reflected results were encoded in a discretionary header field along with the body of a typical Web 404 error response. This way, if anyone discovered the site or replayed my request, they'd just get what looked like an HTTPS error message. Obfuscation wasn't perfect, but it would fool most good IT admins. I'd expect to get responses from all three sites. When my script decoded the response, they all should be similar. If they contained different IP addresses, the script would perform more operations with the knowledge that outbound traffic may be coming through some cloud-based proxy. By this time, the script would have saved the IP addresses to a file.

When done, the next routine would automatically launch, collecting some more inside-out reconnaissance. It initiated what looked like a request for current local weather to Google *Wunderground*. But, in reality, this packet contained the encoded IP address and an additional X-header value that passed the actual IP addresses from Kai's firewall. It worked a bit like a hidden command and control channel allowing me to capture results and inject alternate instructions. If no instructions were returned, my tap would fork a stealth scan of the internal network targeting host identification and port discovery. This scan would creep along at setting T1 and take several hours to complete. Results would be stored on my cloud servers.

SIFTING FOR GOLD

The very next evening, I was just too excited to see the gold my tap snared so I rushed through a plate of crunchy nachos and southwestern tacos that Mum prepared.

"Slow down," Mum said. "Chew your food."

"I'm sorry, I'm in a hurry to study. We have a history test and I'm sure I'm going to ace the thing."

"What's the topic?"

"Magna Carta, King John and the Archbishop of Canterbury."

"You studied that back in Bristol."

"Yup. So, I just need to brush up and I'll ace it." I really didn't like lying to her, but what I really would do was a matter of importance. She just wouldn't understand. Yet.

Shutting my bedroom door behind me, I popped open my history book as well as tapped out a few quick searches online. Shifting to my laptop, I connected to a New York SSL VPN. This would help hide my real IP address in case someone decided to trace the network connections. Next, I connected to my cloud server and opened the Netcat listener. The shells from the tap and server were all stable.

I listed the content of the files on the tap. A full three gigabytes of packet captures waited patiently in a folder along with the scan results. A simple SCP command initiated the transfer to my laptop. Although the command was simple, the large files would take some time to arrive, so I shifted to studying my history notes.

"Hey," Dad poked his head in, startling me. "Is Reba about?"

"Naw. She's out with her folks."

He stepped in, gently shutting the door behind him. The network capture was 18% downloaded and the NMAP file was yet to start.

"Good. Couple things," he soberly said. "Remember our little pursuit and charges against Lesta Andropov?"

I nodded.

"Well, the prosecutor decided not to file charges."

"What? We had him dead to rights. The diamonds. The dognapping. Everything."

"Yup."

Again, I just nodded.

"The district attorney decided that evidence was seized illegally, and he wouldn't file charges."

"But how can that be? Lesta's a real bad guy," my wrist throbbed as it hadn't in several days.

Dad nodded, "There are strict procedures that must be followed. Just grabbing the evidence, starting a fire at the airport, and finding the dog violated the fourth amendment."

I was shocked and could only shake my head.

"This is what I was trying to explain. I needed to keep you and Reba out of this, and my filing paperwork that the evidence was obtained through a confidential informant just wasn't enough. Even if I gave you two up, I don't think the prosecutor would have done anything differently."

"Okay. So, I'll be more careful next time then."

"No, no, no and no again," his voice raised a bit then back to a soft tone. "There won't be a next time. This is dangerous stuff, and these are real bad guys not afraid to harm you kids."

Deflated. That's how I'd describe me now. Deflated with a throbbing wrist. I take one step forward and two steps back. Lesta and the gang were free to pillage.

Dad turned to walk from the room. I just wanted to be alone with my tap now. "Oh," he turned back. "One more thing. I wanted to ask. If you and Reba were into something now, you'd tell me. Right, JP?" He spoke his words carefully.

I felt the temperature in the room drop further. My heart raced. "Yeah, of course," I mustered. Another lie. Lying leads to more lies.

Dad's face was stone cold sober. He flicked his finger on a file he held, then unfolded it and dropped a still photographic image on the table before me. It showed a fuzzy image that could be Reba looking at a camera with the shadow of a person beside her. We had just broken free in the lab. "That kind a looks like Reba, doesn't it?" I said.

"The resemblance is there, but the image sucks. The FBI lab is trying to clean it up," Dad plucked the photo from atop my keyboard. "You'd tell me if you might have been following her into say a secure lab, wouldn't you?"

I looked him straight in the eyes and nodded.

Dad left the room, pulling my door behind him. "I know you will."

Three letters stuck in my mind. F... B... I...

I let out a deep sigh. Aw crap. She had to look straight at the camera. At least my face wasn't visible. But if Dad discovered it was Reba, he'd surely conclude that I was the other figure.

Thank goodness for decrepit closed circuit TV systems. The camera was old, suffering from lens haze, and captured only a grainy, washed-out image that wouldn't support facial recognition. But Dad had to have figured it out, I thought. I couldn't play this game long with him. He was just too crafty.

I texted Reba on her phone: "Call me. 999."

No response. At least not right away.

A soft chime rang. My system had finished downloading the packet capture file from the tap to my cloud server. Now I needed to get that file on my local machine for analysis. I typed a command through the reverse shell instructing the tap to delete the file and start another. Then, I pulled the network packet capture from the cloud system to my local machine and through the SSL proxy. Why such copy functions had a status bar was beyond me. This copy function just dragged. It seemed the status-bar didn't move. In the meantime, I commanded SCP to fetch the internal scan results in an NMAP XML file from the tap. This file was significantly smaller and was on my cloud server in no time at all. As with the packet capture, I routed this file through the SSL proxy to my desktop machine.

The download of the packet capture was well less than 10% complete when the NMAP results arrived on my local machine. There were two, one for a full TCP scan and the other for a UDP scan. I opened the UDP XML file using Zenmap. This was quick and easy to analyze.

Starting with topology view, a network graph of DNS-resolved names. Increasing the ring gap rendered the entire network structure. There were 42 unique devices on the network labeled with IP addresses and name for each endpoint. I picked out the Cisco gateway firewall and saw an adjacent device named "NAS 2304". This was awesome, a networked storage device most likely used for backups and shared files. UDP port 2049 was open for file access. The UDP scan fully resolved the hostname. Another machine with a common system name had an SMB port open. This could be a file server. There were three Apple Macs, IP cameras, and a few MS Windows PCs. The file server appeared as a Windows machine and the IoT devices reported that they were Linux-based.

I opened a second screen to the TCP scan results. No sign of the named NAS device, but the IP address was present that matched the device. For TCP ports, this NAS device had way more than six open communication ports and should be easy to access through my tap if I felt like poking around. It even had port 873-rsync and 2049-NFS_acl open, which I'd expect from a network storage device. But, also having http-80 and https-443 open was a bonus.

Now it was time to look at the network communications captured in the large packet file that just finished downloading. CapLoader popped up displaying the initial net-flow analysis of the packets. Hundreds of thousands of packet headers displayed before me in chronological order. My first approach filtered out noise like NetBIOS, LLMNR, NBNS, SMB, and DNS traffic, reducing the number of packets to 30% of the total.

Even without reading the NMAP scan results, I could see that the network was well organized using a non-routable 10-net scheme. For the moment, I filtered out internal machines talking with other internal endpoints. I was most interested in communications from internal systems to the outside world and, specifically, external IP addresses that were not in the US. This whittled the results down to a few hundred.

There were only 4 hosts on Kai's network that routinely communicated with external IP addresses. One of the addresses was clearly a mail server since the connections were all secured IMAP. My question was which sessions involved the passing of the largest data sets. These could be files, executables, or image objects. I sorted the results and used CapLoader to select the top 22 packets, passing them to another tool, Network Miner. I also noted that the top three packets with the largest data sets were mail attachments routed to Malaysia, Russia, Hong Kong, California and Poland.

"Bingo," I muttered, carving out the files. The file destined for Hong Kong was the PDF document on the chemicals stolen from the lab. A word doc, returning from Hong Kong was in cleartext that was sent about 30 minutes after the mail message with a PDF document. It illustrated several chemical formulas and a process for blending with other elements. Several pages of text were in Chinese and Vietnamese.

"Polliwogs and boxes," as my Dad called them. I copied the first block of characters:

危险。所有化学品的处理必须由合格人员在安全实验室中进行

Good ol' Google translated this as: "Danger. Handling of all chemicals must be performed by a qualified person in a secure lab."

An ominous opening statement.

The Vietnamese block below translated to pretty much the same thing. I snapped photos of the pages that followed and sent them off to Reba. She would know how to read this document.

Scrolling to the last page, I pasted another block from the closing paragraph into Google and read aloud the result: "In the midst of chaos, there is also opportunity. Wings and will of a flying tiger. Fuzanglong."

#

The next day at school I waited by the drive. Reba ran straight over after being dropped off by her pop, "What the heck were those photos you sent me last night?"

I explained what I'd done and where they came from.

"Wazow!" Reba pulled me away from the other students. "I'm not that good with a lot of the very technical terms, but it's a process for blending a set of common chemicals and then using a catalyst for the final preparation. It warns of extreme, caustic danger once a specific catalyst is added and the result is exposed to air. It expands into a very dangerous gas. But I'm no expert in this. My chem is kind of basic and I don't know what all the compounds are referenced in the early pages."

"So, if I make a guess, this could be a series of steps used to make a weapon?"

"Maybe. The instructions reference the serum and blending of all the elements except the final catalyst."

"We're just guessing. These are just theories. We need more facts to support a conclusion."

We walked toward the building.

"And the reference to Fuzanglong?" I asked. "ChatGPT gave me that it's a crouching dragon of hidden treasure that causes seismic disturbances and volcanic eruptions as it moves."

"That's the myth," Reba said. "Given the dragon on Kai's front gate, this could be a moniker used by either Kai or Lesta. The interesting thing is the statement just before that."

"The Sun Tsu quote?"

"Yup." She patted my shoulder and headed off to her first classroom.

I should have told her about the photo Dad had.

After two periods, my mind was stuck on the CCTV image from the lab. It was finally lunchtime, and we met in the library. Reba, with half of a spring roll in her mouth, thumbed through a text and shoved the open page for me to see. She tapped a picture of a great, golden dragon. "This is Fuzanglong," between chews. "The protector of a great fortune beneath the earth. See the giant Pearl in his mouth? It's said he spews volcanic gas on any who challenges or disturbs him. There's a few other terms and words in the text that I don't fully understand: 'tong' and 'kit'."

I typed a few queries into Google and followed with Bing and Yandex searches. The words alone came back with nothing. Then Reba suggested I put them together with a dot. "Tong Yeh-kit," I said realizing that all of the searches returned the same. "He's a dissident in Hong Kong and was sentenced to 9-years in prison."

"So," She pondered aloud. "We have a great dragon protector of the underworld, instructions for cooking up something with a stolen serum, and references to a dissident fighting for Hong Kong suffrage. What's the relation?"

Reba flicked to another text.

"Could Fuzanglong's treasure actually be some reference to winning universal suffrage for the people of Hong Kong?" I asked.

She shook her head, "could just be mythical gobble-de-gook or the sender's ego."

"Given what we know so far," I said. "I really don't like the concept of mass destruction. A serum, mixing chemicals, and reference to Fuzanglong and Yom-kit?"

"Yeh-kit," Reba corrected.

The lunch bell rang. Reba shoved the book back onto the shelf. "I have a free period after this one. I'll research some more and maybe find some useful links. We can get together later after school."

Reba was off to her next class. I still hadn't mustered the courage to tell her about the photo.

After the quick hit using CapLoader and NetworkMiner, I reloaded the packet capture and filtered for email threads on common mail ports. There were a bunch of messages, so I filtered on the word 'Fuzanglong' -- that gave me a single message originating from a Hawaiian IP address. The text listed a few dates just after the next Lunar New Year and mentioned a demonstration that must take place near Diamond Head. There was a single acknowledgement with the word Fuzanglong again. I carved and extracted this mail thread.

I must be missing something more. I reloaded the packet capture extract from the night before when I found the document. This time, I poked at some of the other large files that had been sent. Nothing jumped out at me, so I tried opening the entire Packet capture in Network Miner and set it to identify hosts with zero hops.

It took several minutes to load then gave me a real clear picture of the network endpoints. The listing included most of the IoT devices like printers and cameras.

One of these smaller devices used a camera that dispatched a video file to an external IP. Carving out the video file, I opened it.

The video captured a very fat cat illuminated only by the IR light generated by the camera climbing through the animal door. The camera's view focused only on the animal door, nothing else. If we were standing in the room, it would have seen our legs and feet. Worse yet, it would have captured our faces as we climbed through the door. My heart sank deep into my chest, and I sat back. We could be in real big trouble.

My history exam was less than an hour away, but I needed to follow this up.

The hosts tab on Network Miner gave me some details of the camera. A small wireless device, like the standalone units you get from any online shop. These devices are notorious for going offline or detecting motion, especially after an initial capture. I searched for other video files and only found one other short clip of the cat at a much earlier time.

I breathed a sigh of relief knowing my packet captures spoke the full truth about what crossed the network. Checking the timestamps, I realized the tap wasn't installed when Reba and I entered the house. It didn't have any videos of us leaving, so there's a chance we were not observed.

Nothing I could do now. I shut down my system and quickly reviewed my exam prep notes, then off to history class.

#

By three o'clock that day, I headed home. Reba caught a ride with her mum and big sister. They saw me walking along and stopped by the curb. Reba's mum signaled for me to jump in. CaCee sat in the passenger seat, groaned and rolled her eyes as I climbed in the back with Reba. It was awfully nice of Mrs. Ng to give me a lift.

"I guess the I.Q. in the car just shot up since we picked up nerd-boy," CaCee said as I shut the door.

Reba lashed out and slapped the back of CaCee's head, "Be nice."

"Whatever!" CaCee rubbed the back of her head where Reba made solid contact.

Mrs. Ng asked how I was doing and made idle chitchat as we drove through the neighborhoods and to our houses. I leaned a bit closer to Reba and told her I really needed to talk to her about new information.

Reba just waved her hand silencing me and mouthed the word: "later." Then pointed toward her big sister and mother.

I jumped at an invite from Mrs. Ng to come inside for a glass of punch. She made the best punch, a mixture of mango, pineapple, and orange juice. My house would be empty, and I'd just be having a Coke.

Once inside, CaCee grabbed her bag and left the three of us around the kitchen table. Mrs. Ng poured the punch, then left to fetch the afternoon mail.

"I've got news too, but you go first," Reba said once her mum was out of earshot.

I told her about the video of the cat entering the house but didn't yet tell her about the photo of her in the lab.

"So, did they see us?"

"I don't think so. Can't speak for when we climbed in, but there were no videos of us leaving."

"Let's hope," Reba perked up. "So, today was your odd day, right? You didn't have home room." She spoke about how our class schedules were arranged.

"Yeah."

"Then you don't know about the museum trip?"

"Enough with the 20 questions. What's up?"

She leaned closer. "There's a big field trip coming up for our history classes. We're going to see the dragon exhibition that's on tour from China at the De Young Museum in San Francisco." She smiled and sat back in her chair.

I frowned. "I'm lost. The significance is?"

Reba rolled her eyes. "You idiot. This Lunar New Year celebrates the Year of the Dragon, right? Better still, our school will be making a fieldtrip to the De Young Museum to see the dragon exhibit that's on loan from China."

I frowned again. I was thinking only about the photo from Dad and the possibility we were observed by one of Kai's cameras. The relevance was lost on me.

"Fuzanlong, silly. Sculptures of the other great dragons will be on exhibit too. Now, ask yourself if that trip, the exhibit, and the messages you discovered could have anything to do with whatever Lesta and that big guy we saw might be plotting? Maybe the whole scheme is to steal the dragons and sell them back to a collector in China?"

"Okay. But what does that have to do with the serum and components and a possible weapon?"

Reba looked very deflated.

"It doesn't," I said flatly. "We make conclusions based on facts, not guesses."

She nodded.

"The only thing we can say for sure is Fuzanglong was referenced along with a chemical process involving the serum and some demonstration communicated to someone in Hawaii. And, the demonstration," I popped a couple of air quotes. "Is going to happen in the first few weeks after the Lunar New Year."

"Agreed." She said.

"Oh, and the other thing we know is that Dad has a still photo from the lab with an image that looks like you."

"What?!"

FAMILY TREE

"Chill!"

Mrs. Ng returned at that moment.

"Mom," Reba said, "JP and I are going outside and kick a ball around." She was up and pulling my arm before Mrs. Ng could say much. Never mind I didn't finish my juice.

As we headed out the back door, Mrs. Ng called, "Keep that soccer ball out of my planters."

The door shut as Reba ran out to the center of their backyard where a red and white ball sat. She kicked it bouncing it directly off my chest and back to her, "So, what's this crap about a photo?"

That hurt. She kicked it again, and I proudly stopped it with my knee and foot. "Look. In the lab when the cameras came back online. Just after we got free, they caught a single image of you looking kind a, sort a, at the camera."

"Great," she kicked it back to me. I smacked it back to her, and she unleashed a big, high kick launching the ball over the fence and into my back yard. "How much of me?"

"Sort of from here," I held my hand across my upper lip. "Up to the top of your head."

"JP, that's a crap load." She looked as though she might cry.

"Wait. It's not that bad. The camera is real old and the image was very grainy. Your facial features are not really identifiable and there were no references to your height nearby."

"Have you seen the video?"

"No. Just a single frame blown up to a 5 by 7 print," I approached her reaching out with my arms to give her a hug. She slapped my hand away.

"Can you get the full video?"

I shook my head. "It's in the possession of the FBI."

"FBI?!" her fear turned into rage. "That's even better."

"Their lab is trying to clean the image up, but," I qualified before she could utter the next word, "from what I saw that image won't be easy to clean and there's just not much to work on."

"Hey," Mrs. Ng looked out the back door. "Where's the ball?"

"I kicked it over the fence," Reba said calmly. "Oops." She grabbed my arm. "We're going to go get it."

Following her, I'd say she stomped all the way into my back yard with me in tow. She spun as she entered my yard and stopped.

"What now?" Reba said.

"Say they clean it up and have a clear image," I said. Her eyes widened. "Just say."

"Okay."

"There was other physical evidence left behind in the lab. Remember the tie strips?" She nodded. "Well, mine had blood on them. There's the scissors, too. All that's evidence. They should have collected it all."

Reba crossed her arms and took a couple of deep breaths.

"That evidence will lend support to the fact we were tied up in the lab."

She nodded and looked a lot more relaxed.

"Fingerprints," I said. "On the computer, desk and lab doors."

Her face looked as though she'd kick me, "Stupid. Remember, they all wore gloves. The only fingerprints will be yours and mine."

"Right," I rubbed my forehead for the bit of perspiration forming. "Forgot."

She shook her head. "And you're supposed to be the big-time detective!"

"Blood," I said.

"Yeah, yours from where we were tied up."

"No, no," I waved my hand at her. "Remember the Korean dude? You kicked and broke his nose."

Reba smiled and her eyes sparkled, "Yeah. Got him good with a high kick he wasn't ready for."

"There were probably blood drops over by the door. And there would be micro-evidence as well. Hair. And maybe more."

"Back to my question, now what?"

"I think we have a few choices."

"Let's hear 'em"

"Well," I counted one with my finger held up. "We could come clean with Dad and hope he understands. This one's not too good because he just lost a case against Lesta Andropov that he blames on our Halloween escapade."

"The fire in the hangar probably didn't help that much."

"Yup," I held up two fingers. "We compile the evidence we have up to date and show it to Dad along with the information from the lab."

"That's just like number one. And, as you always say, we have to draw conclusions on facts. Right now, we only have circumstantial evidence that something bad is going to happen."

Now, I nodded agreement, "That leads to three. We keep digging up more evidence until we have a much clearer picture about what's going to happen. Then, we act. If the FBI clean up the picture and it comes to light, then we deal with it at that time having a whole bunch more information."

She sighed deeply. I may have won her over.

"That's our only choice then."

"I can't think of other options unless you have one."

"I wasn't asking. I'm surrendering that we can only do the last option. So, what's the plan?"

I perked up. The worst might be over, "O.S.I.N.T."

"Huh?"

"Open-source intelligence. It's time we got to know our adversaries."

#

We split up, Reba heading to her home, so she didn't run into my Dad at my house. At least not yet. She agreed to start digging for information on Kai-nam. That would be fairly straight forward for her while I took on the other two people. Lesta, Kai's father, and the big guy with the nasty cat allergy.

Once home, I listed out my objectives starting with Lesta Andropov. Who were his friends? What sort of online, digital persona did he have? And where would his digital footprints lead?

Starting with the general search engines, I ran queries on Google, Bing, and DuckDuckGo. Then I got a bit more creative and ran some queries on Yandex. The latter returned several interesting results in Russian that took a bit of work to translate. One particular picture of interest was of two people holding a baby outside in Berlin. The famous wall was covered with people, smashing it into pieces. The face of one was a woman, and the image was quite clear. I captured it and started a Faces search. The other was a man, holding the child. He was young, very fit with huge, muscled arms that tightly stretched his tee shirt.

Another picture popped up of the same very fit man with his arm around a tall, lean boy, probably 10 or 12 years old.

The man wore a slick black sweat suit popular in the 80's with an embroidered emblem above his left breast. I cropped and selected just the emblem, then fed it to an image search tool.

Magnitogorsk wrestling club. Anton Andropov. I searched for the name. Google gave meaningless replies for Yuri Andropov, Secretary General of the Soviet Union. Wrong Andropov, unless Anton was somehow related to the ex-Soviet leader. But that conclusion was a stretch. Translating the name into Russian, I fed it back to Google with the same results. String searching the results, I couldn't find anything about Anton. Next, I searched Yandex.

"Bingo," I said to myself. Anton's career and past fame as a champion Greco-Roman wrestler flooded across the screen. His fame grew in the late 80's, and he would have made the CCCP Olympic wrestling team if it wasn't for a serious hip injury that ended his career. In the past, he was a two-time champion grappling wrestler, a sport popular in the early 80's Russia. I printed the picture of the huge man wearing the traditional black and grey uniform of the Moscow Wrestling Club.

Years after Glasnost and the Motherland's fall, Anton was appointed to lead a European unit of Gazprom. He clearly had very good relations with influential people. Power shifted from the central committee to business leaders. Beyond sports, he must have had a knack for leadership and management. I snipped another picture of him among a group of men at an event in Paris. Around this time, he met and married a French woman who bore a child. They named their boy Lesta, not typically a boy's name and the Russian name was not short for Lester, rather Leicester.

Lesta must wait for now. I continued working through Anton's career and history. Leaving Gazprom just as the Russian government cut energy supplies to the west over a political dispute, Anton registered himself as the managing director of an import/export company out of the Maldives. A year later, he was pictured inside a posh Albanian casino shaking hands with two other men. Seems Anton's company bought a minority stake in the casino. I wondered if he got out of this business by the late 90's when the Albanian economy took a massive downward turn. The next entry was in 2020 when he and his son opened an office and distribution facility out of Long Beach, California. The entity's name had no relation to the one registered in the Maldives, but it's common that a lot of those records may not exist online. Anton's import/export business did very well bringing coffee and teas from far off corners of the globe, along with a healthy list of European antiques, furniture, and jewelry. Most recently, the company exported luxury goods like high-end automobiles to Hong Kong. This caught me as a strong coincidence with the messages my tap had intercepted.

I scribbled a few notes and printed a couple more images about the Long Beach business. Now, onto Lesta Andropov.

As though on queue, the Faces search I began on Anton's wife came back with a single hit on a scanned image from a French paper, a short, terse obituary. She died just days after her only son was born. Whoa, plopped back in my chair. I saw how my Dad felt after my real mum died in a car accident. Even though I was very young, the grief swelled for the woman I never really knew. I actually felt sorry for Anton losing his wife, and for Lesta growing up without a mum. At least my Dad recovered and re-married. There were no suggestions in the intelligence that this ever happened to Anton.

One deep sigh, and I was back at it. I threw the Harvester tool onto Lesta Andropov linked to the import/export company. Then followed links from genealogical birth records in France and forward. Lesta was schooled at a boarding academy outside Bern, Switzerland and then directly into Bern University. I pulled a picture of the skinny, tall young man receiving a trophy at an international chess tournament hosted by the school that had included several Russian chess masters. No sign of his father in the photographs. At least nothing in any of the school photos that were available online. It's like his father left him to be raised by the private school system. I wondered what the two got up to during school holidays and between terms. During this time, there was very little information on Anton Andropov. He was basically a ghost.

Next notable item, US marriage record from Saint Nicholas Cathedral in San Francisco. Lesta married Yun, a Korean woman. I spent a bit too much time searching for images and records relating to this marriage and any ceremony, only to come up with another death certificate eleven months after the birth certificate for a boy, named Kai-nam Andropov. The birth and death certificates were from St. Mary's Medical Center, Long Beach. I printed copies of the marriage, birth and death certificates. This was just too much of a coincidence. My own Mum died when I was young, Kai's mum was lost, and Lesta's mum died in childbirth. I know what I felt and how much I feared automobiles and reckless drivers. But for Kai and Lesta, I wondered how the long-term grief actually manifested itself upon their personalities. This couldn't be answered by Google or public searches. One might think that kids suffering these significant losses might be screwed up and cross paths with the justice systems in countries. Harvester never uncovered any criminal activities or records on Lesta, and Kai seemed clean as a whistle.

Entering Lesta and Kai's home address into the county public tax records, it revealed the lot was purchased just a few months before Kai's birth. The home and land were improved over the next 3 years then they took occupancy. I wondered if Anton actually lived with them in San Jose.

Searching for records related to Anton yielded nothing in the recent years in California. That said, the import/export company was listed as the owner of a 7,000 square foot home along Montcalm Ave in the Hollywood Hills. This home was purchased for just north of a million dollars in the early 2000's. Current tax records listed its value over eight million. Beyond a linkage to Anton's company, there were no records with his name. The import/export company was owned by a chain of LLC's in different states and then to a trust out of Nevada.

I dug further into criminal records and court filings not relying entirely on the Harvester results. In all, the only record was the recent arrest of Lesta by the San Jose Police, but there was a note that charges were dropped. No records throughout state and federal records on Kai, Anton, or the import/export business.

One last, last thing. They had access to an airplane hangar, and I wondered if they had a plane. The US FAA site was a bit of a pain to work with, so I actually started with the European aviation authority. After all, Anton started the business in the Maldives and had ties to the Swiss and French.

Nothing.

Back to the US FAA site. Sure enough, the import/export company was listed as the owner of a Bombardier Global 6000. I printed a picture and wrote the registered tail number on the sheet.

Closing the windows, I opened my own case files and printed a few shots from the warehouse that were captured from my cell phone and drone camera.

Once the printer stopped whirring, I sat for a bit looking at the stack of printed images and notes in the tray. I really wanted to visualize this and put a family timeline together. Any good hacker would do this, so why wouldn't a forensic investigator?

Mum had a perfect roll of blue yarn in her kitchen junk drawer that I retrieved. She'd fallen asleep on the couch with the TV on. She was probably waiting for Dad to return and was so exhausted from her duties at the hospital that she dosed off.

So, I had scissors, yarn and tape. Now I just needed a place to construct the tree. I really didn't want this visible to my parents should they come into my room. It was too big for a chunk of cardboard. Sliding my closet doors back, I pushed the clothing aside looking at the back wall. Not here, I thought. Mum would surely see this, and I could just hear Dad barking after she reported it to him. That's when it struck me, the back of the closet doors. They wouldn't look there.

#

After nearly an hour of work, I stood inside my closet looking at the family montage I'd constructed. Paper, yarn and images were neatly glued to the back of the closet door. I added the final touches, including pictures of the redwood lab, images from that Halloween night with the bag of diamonds, the airport hangar, and the warehouse. Most of these linked to Lesta. The last thing I added was a single sheet from the email that the tap grabbed along with tags marked Hong Kong and Hawaii.

"Well, Lesta." I said aloud. "What are you really up to?"

The closet door slid back, and fright struck my chest. It was just Reba.

"Why are you in the closet talking to yourself?" she said. "Have you lost it or something?"

"How did you get here?"

"Your mom let me in."

"You really gave me a fright."

"Hey, I know. Don't hide in the closet and talk to yourself," she smirked again.

"No, no, no," I stammered. "Come here." I pulled her into the closet and slid the door shut. Flicked on my mini flashlight. "See?"

"Woah. What is this?"

"Family relationships for Kai, Lesta, and Anton Andropov." Starting at the bottom, I walked her through the tree and all of the information I discovered online.

"Where did you get all of this?"

"Public records and a bit of open-source intelligence gathering." I was very proud of what I'd put together in a few hours.

"So, is Anton a Russian oligarch?"

"Not that I can tell. One, I don't think he has that much money and, two, I haven't seen any recent communications or ties back to Mother Russia. This is something we'll watch out for from the tap."

"And both of their wives are dead?"

"No grandmother. No mother. All offspring raised only by men, boarding school bullies and staff."

"It's kind of sad, really."

"But it may explain why they're so hardened."

"And, Kai," Reba asked, "How does he fit in?"

"He keeps a low profile. Nothing in social media, no posts, no messaging beyond what we saw in the Game. I think he was Lulimon in the game arena with Wharf and Sluggo. Even then, I have a feeling he goes to a network outside his home to communicate with friends. The tap has picked up nothing," I pointed to Kai-Nam's picture. "He may just be a tool. Young kid who knows technology. The perfect, trusted nerd to handle the high-tech side of things for the family business."

"The USB drives we discovered back in the warehouse. That could be his handy work?"

"Possibly," I nodded. "He seems fully capable of hacking and stealing digital identities. It would fit."

The closet door slid open. Reba inhaled sharply. My flashlight caught Dad directly in the face. His scruffy unshaven beard and mustache showed just a bit of leftover food as his face transitioned quickly from shock to harsh anger. "What the hell? The two of you in a closet?" His hands blocked his eyes, "And get that torch out of my face."

"It's not what you think," I clicked off the light.

"Your Mum, and your Mum," he glared at Reba. "They'd both flip out. Now, get out of the closet." He motioned for us both to sit on the edge of my bed then stood rubbing his hands over his face, "What were you doing in there?"

Reba blushed as I stammered, "Nothing."

"You know, I really don't want to know. And I really, really don't want to hear any lies."

"I was just working on a project," I waved my hand around the room that was littered with paper scraps, empty tape dispenser, pens, and a partially unraveled ball of yarn.

"Enough," back to the harsh voice. "New rule. When Reba's here, you keep the door open and lights on so I can see you. I just don't need this. Raising one teen is a real pain in the butt. Now, I feel like I've got to watch over you both. Two pains in my butt."

He stepped back. I hoped he'd leave the room. No such luck.

"And you, Reba," he actually spoke in a calm and more normal tone. "Did you have a fun trip to science camp this year?"

Reba nodded.

"Bet you learnt a lot while you were there?" He didn't wait for her to answer, "Do any exploring, like in a lab that's just a quarter mile away?"

Don't look at me Reba, I thought. She stared directly at him, "The forest is a lab of sorts. I learned a whole lot."

I cringed. Don't explode, I thought about Dad and waited for the hammer to fall.

He nodded back to his docile self.

"Funny, that," Dad grinned. "You know, the FBI has a great lab that can deblur and enhance all sorts of images. There were two people caught on a CCTV camera during a burglary. I really hope it wasn't the two of you, otherwise you may have to do some explaining to a much higher authority than me."

"Mum?" I asked.

He frowned at me, "Not that high of an authority. Just the FBI." He stepped out of the room pushing my door wide open against a pile of books, "This stays open. Lights on. Oh, and clean this mess up."

Reba and I let out sighs of relief. Then she started laughing, "I wonder what he thought we were doing in the closet?"

FUZANGLONG ROARS

Diamonds, Serum & Dragons

Just another day at school. No pending exams. Grades were posted, and midterm boredom set in. Teachers focused on bringing up the bottom 50% of the class in subjects like history and algebra but not needed for me.

Yesterday, I launched a control script and placed it on my cloud platform. The script logged into the tap at Lesta's home and extracted the latest network packet capture file, removing it from storage and running Zeek on the capture. Zeek parsed the dense log files producing a verbose set of categorized logs that pulled connections, weird stuff, mail, and gave references to any and all files.

I sat at my usual table in the library, laptop open and set in motion an analysis script that produced a histogram of the connections. This output listed the top 30 network connections by both IP address and URL. It also extracted any passwords and authentication credentials that were found.

In most cases, the passwords were encrypted, and authentication was covered by transport security. Yesterday's dump had a couple of clear passwords used to access file shares and systems that were on the other side of a VPN tunnel, probably the Long Beach offices of the Import/Export company.

But the important analysis was from the filtered connection log that showed all independent communications to and from internal to external network addresses. The filtered list then counted the number of connections to the various addresses allowing me to see if the total number was increasing or decreasing over time. Yesterday, the number of connections into and out of Hong Kong were up a total of 30%, well over a few standard deviations of the usual average. Up until now, the traffic volume fluctuated each day well less than a single deviation from the average. The spike was more than likely a sign of something to come.

Digging deeper into the network traffic, I ran Bulk Extractor against the entire packet capture. This only took a few minutes to complete, carving out all objects contained in the capture to separate files based on their identity. There were several picture images that had been sent. Using Explorer, I viewed the images as thumbnails, allowing me to scan through them quickly. Two of the files jumped out at me. One was a mapped location of the De Young Museum in the heart of San Francisco's Golden Gate Park. The other was a warehouse on the waterfront near the container docks and Hunters Point.

Coincidence? I thought not.

I ran a tool to view the extended information contained in them. They were both extracted from the same mapping tool and created only minutes apart. This started me examining the other files and images that had been extracted. A picture of a golden dragon clutching a huge pearl in its left claw caught my eye. The dragon was alone on a white background. The extended information about the dragon showed a few interesting facts. It too had been copied from some site, and then the file had been modified. Unlike the others, the timestamps were all consistent with a straight copy of the object and then sent across the network. This one reported modification some 15 minutes after the initial copying. Fortunately, the extended data reported the location from which the file originated.

Popping open a Tor-enabled browser, I went to the site and found the original image. I copied it to my machine and calculated an MD5 hash. Next, I calculated the same hash on the file extracted from the packet capture. They didn't match. "Go figure," I whispered to myself.

I would normally have opened a hex editor on the extracted file, but time was now important. I only had 10 minutes before my next class, and I couldn't be late for history with Mr. Thompson. He flipped out whenever any student was late. So, I just ran the strings utility against the image file. There were two ASCII-text strings that flowed out of the image, the first was "03:10 Nov 20" and "04:00 Nov 20". The 20th was two days away or the day after our class trip to the museum.

Had to go. I closed my laptop, packed up and headed to class.

#

I found Reba outside on a bench near the great oak tree in the school courtyard. The temperature was cool and skies clear.

I went through everything I'd observed earlier in the packet capture from my tap.

"The times don't really make sense," I said between mouthfuls of my favorite bologna sandwich. "Why hide them inside an image file?"

"You're sure about the extraction and values that you pulled?"

"Yup," I said.

Reba paused for a moment, then frowned. "What if the times are in Hong Kong's time zone?"

I started counting on my fingers.

"Don't," Reba covered my hands with hers. "Three AM in Hong Kong would be noon, here."

"UTC," I said with a bit of a spark. "Oh-three-ten UTC is eight-ten PM here on the day before."

We both smiled.

"Right in the middle of our field trip to the museum."

"And oh-four hundred would be nine PM the day prior."

Not only had steganography been used to hide the dates and times, but they were also passed as a universal time coordinate.

"We'd best be on our guard at the museum," Reba said. "We're supposed to get there around seven PM."

"And Dad?" I asked. "Should I tell him something's up?"

Reba shook her head. "We don't really know anything, right? He's going to be one of our chaperones on the trip and we can get him if something bad goes down."

#

The next evening, Dad sat across from Reba and me in the next to last row of the clunky school bus roaring up the 280 freeway. Even at 55 miles an hour, the bus lacked suspension and the seat springs cushioning my butt felt like they'd come through at any minute.

"What a reeky spot," Dad pinched his nose, looking at us.

The diesel fumes were actually pretty strong, and I just nodded, flashing a grin. Kai sat up near the front of the bus with one of his buds. For me, watching Kai was far more important than gassing with Dad. A sense of foreboding wouldn't leave me. I didn't sleep well the night before and kept going over the network data in my brain. Something awful was coming. The image of the dragon staring down at visitors from the gates at Kai's home just wouldn't go away either. Diamonds, serum and dragons. I really hated keeping things from Dad, but he'd flip out if I told him all the evidence I had. No less, I'd have to confess to Reba and me being the subjects in the CCTV image from the lab. Not good. I convinced myself the only way out was to let happen whatever was going to happen tonight. I shut my eyes. Diamonds, serum, and dragons. I clicked my heels.

"Cool it, JP." Reba saw me. "Aren't you excited to see the great dragons?"

"Sure."

"This is one of the biggest and best things to be doing. We really get to see them." She was a bit too effervescent. Too many bubbles. She was more excited than when she scored a football goal on the jay-vee squad at school.

At half past seven, the bus hissed to a stop behind a row of similar buses. Clearly, we weren't the only school visiting the museum during this special show. The museum would usually be closed, but tonight it was just hosting high schools from around the area. There had to be twenty or more buses in the parking lot. We all stood to file out of the bus as the front doors swung open. Mr. Thompson, the Vice Principal and my history teacher, led the class from the bus. Dad was the sweep man making certain none of us were left behind.

"My day off." Dad motioned for us to walk in front of him. "And I agreed to chaperone a bunch of tweeners on a field trip."

"It'll be fun, Detective Palmer," Reba bubbled stepping into the aisle. "It will be educational as well," she jumped a bit. "It's the only time that the golden Fuzanglong will be visiting our city. It's a real honor before the Lunar New Year and a gift tour from the Chinese government."

Reba turned, facing Dad. "Did you know that dragons are much more than mythological creatures to Asian people? Their snake-like bodies, long horns, and mustache-like whiskers bring luck and prosperity. I hope we get to touch one. I really, really do. They fly using magic."

"Fuzanglong," she went on, "is one of the most revered of the dragons. Protector of precious stones and minerals. It's said that he creates volcanic eruptions when disturbed or as a means of protecting his continent."

"Volcanoes," Dad rolled his eyes. "Great. That's all I'd need."

Mr. Thompson held up a bright yellow folder over his head signaling that the class should rally around him. All the students fell quiet. Mr. Thompson was not someone to mess with. Even Reba was scared of him. And I certainly was as well. Dad, I could handle, but Mr. Thompson was an entirely different matter. Although very soft spoken, his words fell on deaf ears only once. He was quick to dole out detention, much less suspensions and full expulsions. After all, remember Sluggo and Wharf, they were dropped off at the bad kid's school across town. That's where all troubled kids ended up as a last chance to get their high school diplomas. As for Reba, me and the rest of the class, we wanted nothing to do with bad kid's school.

Once the group stopped shuffling and stood still looking up at the six-foot six pole that was Mr. Thompson, he handed out pages from the folder. "We're doing this visit as a treasure hunt" he said. "You'll team up with two other people of your choosing and find all the items based on the clues in the hunt. We let you all keep your cell phones just for this. Use your phones to take pictures of each item and describe the significance of the legend or story along with the item, then turn it in via email."

Reba snatched the sheet when it came close and pulled me into her group. "We need one more," Reba said looking around at the other students.

"How about Gina?" I chirped. Gina was the cutest girl in our history class.

Reba frowned at me. I felt the temperature drop 20 degrees as she punched my shoulder hard. "Not your type," she snapped. "Hey, Kai! Over here!" Reba called, still holding her attention on me.

I grinned.

Kai strolled over to Reba holding his hands in his pockets. "Yeah?"

"Join our group. JP and me."

He glanced my way, then back to Reba. "Totes."

"Awesome," I thought aloud then felt Reba's heel dig into my big toe through my loafers.

I glanced past Kai toward the front of the museum. Leaning against a pillar near the lowest step was Lesta, Kai's Dad. I couldn't believe my eyes.

"What's up with you?" Kai asked me.

My attention snapped to him, "Nothing. Nothing at all."

"Reba was about to tell us what the first objective is and you're staring off somewhere."

"No, I wasn't," my protest felt hollow. I glanced back over to the steps leading up to the museum's main entrance. Lesta was gone. I looked around.

"Hey!" Kai chirped. "Nerd-boy. Stay with us." It's like he knew what I'd seen and was distracting me back to the treasure hunt, "Go on, Rebecca."

"Right," she read the sheet, then aloud. "This dragon was the first symbol of Chinese federal authority dating back to 189 AD."

"The yellow dragon?" I guessed. After all, it was the symbol on the national Chinese flag for a few centuries.

"Good one," Kai said.

"Not old enough, though," Reba said. "The answer must be Yinglong. The first and only winged dragon."

"Okay," Kai said. "Let's check this out."

He strode off, leading us to the front steps of the museum. I held Reba back a bit and whispered that I'd seen Lesta standing by the right side of the stairs we just stepped on.

"Are you sure?" Reba asked.

I nodded.

"Then it's good we're keeping our enemy close to us," she motioned toward Kai who was well up the steps.

"I don't like this," I said.

"Best we can do and hope for. Now, let's do some dragons," She sprang up to the top of the stairs while I trudged behind. Man, I didn't like the empty feeling in my stomach that something really bad was about to happen.

At the top of the steps, I turned slowly to look down on the people ascending behind us and in the park area across from the museum. I studied each face, but no Lesta. Maybe I just imagined he was there.

"JP!" Reba shouted from the security line.

I turned and joined her.

Passing through the metal detector and the bag inspection, my backpack got tugged by the guards. No way I could bring my bag into the museum. They pointed me to a coat and bag check off to the left, and I ran over and dropped off my bag. Guess they don't want computers or drones in the museum. I re-entered the security line and completed screening.

"Nice of you to join us," Kai said. "Shall we go to the exhibit?" he motioned toward the special events hall.

I followed Reba and Kai into the hall. The walls were done in gold, crimson red and charcoal black. Two large lights highlighted the head of a huge dragon grinning to greet people entering the hall. Reba led the way through the initial exhibit to a case holding a tiny jade dragon with the common four legs and five clawed feet resembling eagle claws. But this small dragon had tiny wings over its pair of front legs.

"This must be the first find," she pointed at the dragon. "Yinglong, around 200 AD and the Han Dynasty." She snapped a picture with her cell phone and texted it to the email address Mr. Thompson provided in the instructions.

"Are you sure?" I asked.

"She's right," Kai interjected. "See the tiny wings in the carving. It's the only dragon with wings. It was a symbol of federal authority during the dynasty."

Reba nodded, "That's correct."

"What's our next clue?" I asked.

"The first instruction was only to find this dragon and the information would lead us to the next," Reba studied the contents in the case.

A placard described a timeline and information on where the artifact was discovered. Not far from the discovery of the terracotta army outside of Beijing.

"So, thoughts on the next clue?" Kai asked.

I watched Kai closely. He just rolled back on his heels and stuck his hands in his pockets. "There must be a clue here to the next," I said.

"There is," Reba said. "Yinglong became a symbol of the Han Dynasty."

"And here," I said pointing at the display. "It says Yinglong had the power to control the skies. So, storms maybe?"

Reba grinned, "That's it. Yinglong was replaced as the symbol of federal power after the Song Dynasty and was replaced by the common yellow dragon." She looked around.

"Over there," Kai said pointing to an exhibit a row away. It displayed a bright yellow, snake-shaped dragon. Of course, he'd know about dragons given his home had a huge one guarding the gate.

"There are two dragons depicted here," Reba said. "The first, on the left portion of the exhibit is Yinglong, the winged dragon in flight. Next to it is an ancient stone script that's been translated to explain that great wars fell over the country when Yinglong encountered Huanglong, the yellow dragon. Many thousands lost their lives over the following centuries of civil wars until feudal states were unified under the Jin dynasty into what is mostly the China we know today.

In that time, the yellow dragon became the symbol of Imperial China," Reba snapped a few pictures.

"We need the next clue," I said.

"Hey," Kai called us over to the next case. "Read this." The case housed several stone symbols of dragons in circles. "Huangdi, known as the yellow emperor, was said to be related to Shennong and dragons. His symbol was the yellow dragon. He had it carved all over his palace and stone dragon heads were shaped on stair rails."

"The myth," Reba added. "Claims Huangdi was immortalized as a dragon upon his death." Reba paused, looking around rather frantically.

"What is it?" I asked, still keeping an eye on Kai.

"That's the next clue."

"What is?" Kai asked.

She gave him a harsh glance, "In the latter Qing dynasty, the dragon was yellow and the symbol of imperial, federal power. As the Ming Dynasty rose, the dragon became red."

"So, we need to find the red dragon?"

"Yup," she pointed toward the entrance to a second hall where the entrance was flanked by two great red dragons grinning from their fanged jaws. "This way."

Inside, the path through the exhibit was lined by a blood red, glowing dragon's body. A single, understated bench atop a pedestal was the dragon throne of the Ming Dynasty. Another class moved away from the throne, leaving us as the only ones for a moment.

"This can't be the real, I mean the real, dragon throne," Kai said. "No way."

Reba and I read the information placard. "He's right," I said.

"It's a replica of the throne based on early texts," Reba said.

"Then," Kai stepped over the ropes surrounding the display. "I shall sit upon the throne."

As his butt rested on the gold bench, alarms whined.

"What the heck are you doing?" Reba yelled.

"Get off that thing," I ordered.

Kai just took out his cell phone and began snapping selfies of him seated on the imperial throne. His face and eyes were locked on mine.

Two security guards appeared demanding that Kai leave the throne and cross the ropes. But he just sat there taking pictures and his stare fell cold upon me. The guards gave him one more warning, then quickly crossed into the exhibit where they flanked him and grabbed his arms. Kai was no match or problem for the two burly guards that hoisted him from the seat and away through a side door.

"Your Dad's going to be real pissed off about this," Reba said in his wake.

"That was staged."

#

"Did you see?" I said to Reba. "His stare locked onto me. He never took his eyes off of me."

"You're paranoid," Reba said.

"Even when they took him back through the doors, he turned and looked directly at me."

"JP," Reba hauled back to hit me when I looked away from the door where Kai was taken and back to her. She sighed and relaxed. "I guess we need to find your Dad or Mr. Thompson."

I nodded, "Agreed."

We walked back through the first exhibit, "You're out of it tonight," she continued. "First you think you see Lesta. He's not there. Then Kai does something stupid and gets hauled off because he's a jerk. And now, you somehow think he's focused on you and playacting."

At that moment, the fire klaxon sounded in the museum. Strobe lights flashed all around. An epileptic student from our school dropped, convulsing from a seizure. Security guards pushed through the crowd forming around him. Reba and I froze watching the growing mayhem before us. An announcement for everyone to "calmly" exit the museum was clearly ignored as a few hundred people rushed for the exit as a cloud of white smoke billowed from the exhibit room. Screams. And more screams. Groups of students and chaperones pressed toward the exit. Reba and I were bumped back against a wall. Dad appeared grabbing Reba and my arms. "Let's go!" He said.

"No!" I pulled back against him. "This is all fake."

"What?!" he yanked us into the flow of humans heading for the door. "How do you know?"

"I just do."

"Detective Palmer," Reba shouted and pulled against him. "JP may be right. Just before the alarm. We saw Kai do something real stupid with an exhibit."

"So!" Dad pulled against both of us.

"Kai was taken away by two security guards. They were both big wrestler-types. I think I know one of them from a week or so ago when I broke his nose. They work for Lesta."

Dad relaxed and looked at Reba.

"I slipped a tracker into Kai's coat pocket when we boarded the bus tonight. At least let me check to see where he is."

"Okay but hurry up."

I activated an app on my phone. The tracker alerted that it was in the museum parking lot. "No, no, no. This can't be right," I said.

"Let's get out of here," Dad yanked our arms.

"Kai has to be in the museum. He must have found the tracker and slipped in the seat of our bus."

Reba and I pulled against his strength to no avail, and we soon were outside and down the steps. Mr. Thompson stood with a group of kids.

"Thanks, Stafford," Thompson said as we approached. "We got two more."

"Do you have everyone?" Dad said.

"All but one."

Dad glanced at Reba and me, then asked, "Kai-nam?"

"Yup," Thompson said, nodding his head.

Dad loosened his grip on Reba and me. He moved us away from the center of the group to stand out of earshot. "Alright, be quick," he said hoarsely. "What do you two know?"

"I told you. Kai was pulled out by two fake security guards just before the alarms went off," Reba said.

Dad wasn't buying Reba's statement. I knew he needed more information and now was the time.

"Stop," I said. "There's more Dad."

Reba's expression devolved into a look of terror.

"Something big is going down tonight here in Frisco. Kai, Lesta and Anton Andropov are up to their necks in it."

"And you know of Anton, how?"

Reba's eyes widened.

"For now, just believe that I do. And we know about the stolen serum from the Redwood Lab."

"Rubbish!" Dad slapped his forehead. "I knew you guys were involved in this mess."

"We're not involved," Reba protested, but Dad just waved the palm of his hand at her.

"Give, JP," Dad prompted.

"Look, after the diamond case with Lesta, I built a family tree to understand how various people are involved. While doing this, I kind of intercepted communications that led me to believe something big is going down tonight. Here! In San Francisco!"

"The museum? A heist?" Dad asked.

"No," I shook my head. "Everything happening right now may just be a smoke screen or somehow involved with activity coming out of Hong Kong."

"If they grab the dragons, it will raise a hell of a hullabaloo with China."

"That's true, JP," Reba interjected. Dad just stared at me.

"Doesn't fit with the other information we've captured. There's something much bigger going down and it involves the serum. I only wish my tracker was still in place on Kai."

"Okay," Dad clearly had a plan as he no longer stared at me and looked around. "I'm going to get in the museum and find Kai." He pulled his police badge holder from his pocket. "You two stay here," He turned to Mr. Thompson. "I'm going to find Kai." Then, off he dashed toward the door the fire crews and police controlled. We saw him show his badge to an officer and speak to one of the security guards. The alarms screeched from within the museum. I watched as Dad spoke to one of the security staff that held a radio. He spoke on it and then shook his head. I told him Kai was taken by some fake security guys, but he wouldn't believe me.

Dad ran back over to Reba and me. "You're right. Kai wasn't taken by the real security."

"Told ya' so," I said. Reba grinned.

"Knock it off, smarty." He looked around, then asked. "What do you know? Tell me."

"I need my equipment, inside at the coat check."

"Right, stay here." Dad ran back to the guard he'd spoken with. The two of them went into the museum.

"What will you tell him?" Reba asked.

"After I check a couple things. There're three possible sites where an exchange or something might go down. I'll give him that."

"Nothing about the lab, right?"

"He doesn't need to know about that. It's irrelevant now."

Dad returned with my pack, and I removed my laptop. "I need somewhere to sit or work." I said.

Dad nodded then turned to where Mr. Thompson stood with the other kids. "Mr. Thompson," he called as he grabbed Reba by the shoulder. "I'm going to take them to the medics to get checked out. She was in the smoke."

Reba coughed a few times.

"Good idea, Stafford," Thompson replied.

The three of us walked quickly to the other side of a gravel path to where two ambulance crews had set up a triage area. Just beyond them, there were three rows of picnic tables in a grove of neatly manicured sycamore trees with an amphitheater stage at the far end. Beyond, was a grassy knoll that must have been crowded on nice spring and summer evenings for concerts in the park. I sat along the first table. Reba joined me. My computer opened and booted on the table, and Dad with one foot rested on the bench across from us.

Once on, I popped open a document file that I'd captured notes on and extracted a map. The map identified 4 locations, one of which was the de Young Museum. The other three locations were on the bay front. These all had been described in communications between Lesta and a mail alias in Hong Kong over the past few days. One was to be chosen. The problem was which wharf and container dock was it? I spun the machine around so Dad and Reba could see the screen.

"There are three areas along the waterfront that are candidates," I pointed to the screen. "Two in Bayview-

Hunters Point and one along China Basin. The meet up must be scheduled at 9 PM."

"It's 8:20 now. That's not much time to figure out which of these. What are they exchanging."

"They referred to the breath of Fusanglong."

"Gas," Reba muttered, then straightened looking at Dad. "They must have processed the serum into a gas and they're selling it."

"What?" Dad said.

"Fusanglong is said to breathe dangerous green gas as a last effort to protect the treasure from mortals. Aside," she added casually, "from the dragon's ability to launch volcanic eruptions and earthquakes."

"Oh, this is just great," defeat in my Dad's voice. "So, I'm supposed to scramble SWAT teams to all three of these locations based on some dragon legend and information from two kids?"

"I'm telling you that it's happening," I pressed. "You said yourself that the FBI was looking into the redwood lab matter. Call them."

He shook his head, "There are rules. I can't just call the FBI." He dropped his butt on the other bench. The picnic table lurched enough that Reba grabbed onto the edge of the table and grabbed the laptop. "I could get laughed off the force for this. Worse yet, I could be assigned the underground detail forever and ever."

"Underground detail?" Reba asked softly. I grabbed the back of her hand and shook my head that she shouldn't ask.

"Look, Dad," I said. "We can find them and summon backup later."

"It's just not worth it, JP," he looked at us. "I can't put the two of you in jeopardy."

As Reba spoke again trying to convince him to do something, I concentrated on logging into the tap at Kai's house. The museum WiFi signal was too far away, but there was an open WiFi in the grove where we sat. Probably available for people to use while having lunch in the park. In a few moments, I was online and connected to my tap. I downloaded the current network captures and processed them with Zeek and my script. Before examining the output, I loaded the capture into Network Miner. About two hours ago, an email had been sent by Lesta that contained a Word document as an attachment. It was sent to the same mail address in Hong Kong. Extracting the attachment, I attempted to open the document. It was AES encrypted. The AES key was encrypted and combined with a password. If Lesta was sending an encrypted document, then he must have had a way to send the password. I sorted all of the emails by send time that were from Lesta. Anyone sending an encrypted document to another person must have had a way to send the password. Lesta may not have sent it directly to the receiver of the document. He could send it to an alias or someone else. Sure enough, not 2 minutes after he shipped out the mail with the encrypted document attached, then he sent another email to a strange looking name made up of a 20-character string at monkeymail.com. I tried opening the encrypted document using the 20-character string as the password. No go. That would have been just too easy.

The text of the message said the password to the document was the name of a close, mutual friend.

"Look," Reba stood pointing across the park. "It's Lesta and the two goons that acted like security guards."

Dad stood and I spun to have a look. There he was with the two guys following him. They disappeared onto a path leading into a dense grove of Eucalyptus trees. One of the main roads away from the museum was just beyond the grove.

"Damn," Dad said. "Let's get after 'em." We stood and I packed away my equipment. "STOP!" Dad exclaimed. "We can't. Thompson and the parents will go nuts."

"So go tell them," I said. "Reba and I will follow them and report back."

"Damn," Dad turned. "Go, go, go. Call me." He ran back to the other side of the ambulance where Thompson and the other students mustered. Reba and I ran across the grove to the trail where they had last been seen.

THE EXCHANGE

The trail wound through stands of Eucalyptus and emerged onto a sidewalk along a main road. A taxi stand was just down about 50 yards to the left. We walked that direction and gazed into the windows of each car. A black stretch limousine passed driven by one of the fake museum guards. Reba stopped and turned to say something. I grabbed her shoulder and pulled her toward the taxi stand. We jumped into a bright yellow Toyota Prius driven by a polite Punjabi fella. "Follow that limo," I shouted after stuffing Reba and myself into the taxi.

"Oh, right? Follow the car, he says."

I grabbed a C-note from out of my backpack and slapped it on the console between the front seats, "It's our parents. And, keep the change, just don't lose 'em."

"You're the boss." He threw the car into gear and swung into traffic cutting off a white 'burb that honked at us. He gunned the little hybrid, and it actually accelerated as he ducked in and out of traffic. Reba and I bounced side to side in the back seat.

"Ohhhh, betta put your seatbelts on," the driver said peeking in the mirror. "You two don't seem related."

"Step. . ." Reba and I said together. Then I finished. "She's my stepsister."

Reba frowned hard at me and whispered, "I have to be the evil stepsister?"

I just smiled as he cut a hard right turn.

"Hey," I yelled. "How do you know he went this way?"

The Indian driver grinned in the mirror. "It only makes sense as a route that they'd turn here," He swung the wheel dashing around two cars along the three-lane road. "See." He nodded toward the vehicle that was two cars ahead. It was the limo.

"This is fine. Don't get too close."

"You don't want your parents to know you're here then?"

Reba and I looked at each other. "That's right," I said.

#

After a few more turns and climbing a steep San Francisco hill, the limo pulled to the corner of a hotel on California Street. The back door opened, and Kai emerged to stand by the open door. No one else got out of the car. Our driver pulled to the side of the curb across from the limo.

"Guess we're here," the driver said.

Reba and I didn't move.

"Not so fast," Reba said pointing to the exit of the hotel. "It's Anton."

The man emerging was huge. Shoulders and arms the size of my legs, no neck, and a massive chest and thin waist. Just what I'd expect of a pro wrestler. A truly frightening sight if you were on the wrong side of his anger.

"Whoa," the driver exclaimed. "Your papa is a real big man."

"Yup."

Anton folded himself into the back of the limo followed by Kai, who pulled the door shut in his wake. The limo pulled away from the curb and roared down California Street following one of the famed San Francisco cable car lines. Our cab driver sat motionless.

"Can you follow him?"

"Oh, yes. I could."

"Well?" Reba added. "Look. That guy they picked up is a very bad guy. He's going to hurt a lot of people."

The driver just stared at us in the rearview mirror. Reba looked at me. I pulled out the last C-note that I had in my emergency money and set it on the center console.

"That man," the driver said, "must be very bad." He grinned flashing the pearly white teeth as he glanced at the money and then back to the road. "Hang on." The cab swung a U-turn from the curbside parking and accelerated down the hill. The traffic light at Powell Street was just changing as our driver punched it, launching the front two wheels a few inches off the ground as our Prius crested the edge of the hill. We slowed at Montgomery Street and gently approached the rear of the limo. We stopped just as the limo's rear tires spun into a right turn and accelerated down Sansome Street.

"Now that just upsets me," our cabbie said. Reba and I looked at one another as the driver reached deep under the dash of the Prius. "Hold on," The driver gunned the engine as our front tires spun on the pavement, and we turned to follow. "My cousin made a couple of modifications to this car," he said as we lurched down the street. Reba and I pressed back into our seats. My stomach was somewhere in my throat. I felt sick, the world spun with us, and I wanted to throw up. I glanced at Reba just as we bounded over a hump, keeping pace with the limo. She smiled huge and actually said "weee" once.

After passing over an old draw bridge, our cab slowed. "They're gone. Must have turned off somewhere." We took the first left turn and meandered down the short street to the end. At the end of the street, the cab came to a stop just at a sharp right turn where the street left the Pier 90 area and headed to the container terminal in Pier 96.

"I'm sorry, guys." The driver said. "Seems they just disappeared."

"Or you lost them," Reba snapped. She grabbed one of the C-notes from the center console.

"I don't really care. You two can get out of my cab at any time now."

Reba flopped back in the seat.

"Where is 500 Amador Road?" I asked.

He turned a quick U in the center of the street and stopped only a few hundred feet on in front of the Cemex Pier 92 cement plant.

"You've arrived," the driver said as he snatched the remaining 100-dollar note from the center console.

The plant was illuminated only by the lights hung on the side of the structures. Lots of belts, rock crushers, and piles of dusty grey powder. Reba and I exited the cab. As soon as the passenger door closed, the driver floored it, lurching away from the plant, curb, and our lives.

"Well, this is nice," Reba said looking around as a gate opened and two long trucks hauling cement rambled over potholes and onto the street.

"It's one of the addresses that were included in the messages from Lesta to the people in Hong Kong. And look over here," I motioned to a small puddle of mud just beyond the road. Look at the tire tracks on the other side. "That's about the width of a Cadillac limo, right?"

Reba studied the ground. "Certainly not the tracks from one of the trucks we see out here."

"Come on," I led us toward the automatic gates. "We need to get inside."

We didn't need to wait too long. Just as we reached the large, corrugated steel automatic gates, a bell rang out and the gates drew open. Reba and I slid around to the other side and walked along where the gate was actually opening. Another cement trucks rounded an inner corner and lumbered out the gates.

My phone rang. It was Dad.

"Hello," I said.

"Don't you hello me," Dad shouted. "Where the heck are you?"

"We followed Kai and Lesta."

"Well, you didn't follow Lesta. He's standing right in front of me talking to Mr. Thompson."

"How can that be?"

"Lesta is signing Kai out and off the trip like a good parent. Says Kai's grandfather showed up in Frisco last night and wants to grab a late supper."

"What's going on?" Reba nudged my side. I gave her the palm of my hand and pushed back.

"Dad, I'll tell you we followed Kai and Anton then."

"Andropov?" Dad's voice was a harsh whisper. If Lesta was with him. I could imagine him stepping back from Mr. Thompson and the others.

"Yeah, the big guy." I said. "Kai took a limo from the museum to the Huntington Hotel on California and picked up the big guy, Anton. Now we're down around Pier 96 at the Cemex cement plant."

"Holy Lord."

"Dad, Dad, don't flip out. Reba and I are safe. We're watching the activity. Look. I'll switch on share my location with your phone. Then you will know where we are."

"Bloody hell! Fine. Look, JP. You two stay put. I'll sign you both out so Thompson and the other students can get back home. Then I'll meet up with you. Okay?"

"Yeah," I said nodding at Reba.

"JP, just stay put. And another thing," Dad said. "Someone stole one of the display dragons, fake gold, and about 3 feet long. Not much of this makes any sense. Stay put."

Beep. Connection dead.

"Look! Over there!" Reba pointed.

Kai walked from a small office building and climbed up the side of one of the conveyer belts that hauled gravel and rock to a crusher. He stopped on a platform about halfway up and held a small device up to his eyes. He slowly scanned the area with the device.

"Take cover!" I pulled Reba behind two large containers that backed up to the perimeter wall.

"What?"

"Infrared," I said. "Kai's scanning the area for biological life forms. We can't stay here. We have to get inside. Somewhere. That device can probably see our reflective halos behind this container."

Reba pushed past me and toward the far corner of a container, "There's a building entrance about 30 yards away."

I scooted next to her, "Now, all we need is a diversion."

The bell on the gates rang in the distance as an empty cement hauler returned to the plant. The truck rumbled in casting a huge white dust cloud in its wake. "This is it, now!" We jumped to our feet and ran from the cover into the dust storm behind the truck all the while holding course on the door we'd seen. Our course was perfect, and we both reached the door. She pulled it open, and I followed her inside.

We hunched over our knees gasping for breath after a dust storm sprint. Reba coughed a few times and then we both stood straight. The inside was illuminated by two bare light bulbs. Coats, boots and tools hung along the walls and there was a dirty glass wall that looked into machine areas deeper in the plant.

"Over there," Reba pointed to a far corner of the room. It was an opening in the floor with a steel set of stairs descending into an area below. We climbed down slowly, conscious of the sounds our feet made on the steel rungs. As we stepped off, there were steam pipes, a lot of hissing from machinery, and more dust.

"What now?" I asked.

"This way, there's a corridor connecting to somewhere over there." Reba was off and jogging at a gentle pace. She leapt onto a small platform at the entrance to a cement tunnel. I followed. "Come on." She waved. And we're off into a dimly lit tunnel filled with lingering dust particles that seemed to float in space in our wake. Reba slowed as we approached the end of the tunnel. It connected to a much larger room. Voices. We could hear voices in the room. Reba stopped by the edge of the tunnel, her back to the wall. I slid in beside her.

"What is it?" I asked.

"I think they're just over to the right," Reba said. "There's no real cover if we leave the tunnel."

I activated the video recorder on my cell phone and held my arm out to capture a 180-degree view of the chamber ahead of us. Three men stood beside a pop-up card table that held a box-like glass chamber, a computer, and what looked like chemical test equipment. Panning to the other side of the room, there was an elevator and large motors and machinery that ran the rock crusher that was just above us. The crusher was not in use, otherwise we wouldn't be able to hear anything.

Ding. The elevator bell sounded. I activated the video capture and held my phone out again. It was the big guy, Anton, and Kai, flanked by the same two guys that were fake security officers in the museum. One of the men carried a chrome briefcase. They approached the three men standing behind the card table.

The man at the card table stripped off his jacket and rolled up his white shirtsleeves, exposing a large red and green dragon tattoo on the inside of his forearm. He meticulously folded his jacket and set it over a case that was by his side. He slipped on a white lab coat and snapped on a pair of blue gloves. The scientist-looking guy was the first to speak, "You brought the sample?"

"And," Anton spoke softly, "you have the agreed funds?"

The scientist waved to his accomplices. They stacked two suitcases on the table, opening them to flash a whole lot of cash.

Anton nodded, "We carefully packed one of the vials in the jaws of this dragon." He waved an order to the goon that carried only a velvet sack. He extracted a golden dragon and held it, so the mouth was facing the scientist.

"You're not beyond taking significant risks, I see," The scientist said.

"We do what's necessary." Anton set the dragon model onto the table.

"The catalyst and other serum vials are in the case," Anton motioned toward the case carried by goon number two. "I thought the dragon tong would appreciate a presentation of the great Fuzanglong."

Reba's watch perked up. "I found this on the Web. Fuzanglong, a mythical Chinese dragon."

"Shut up, Siri." Reba slapped at her wrist.

"See what that was," Anton barked. Kai and one of the goons moved toward our tunnel.

That was it. We ran as hard as we could back through the tunnel. Reba reached the metal ladder at the other end and stepped by the side of it. "You first, JP."

I didn't need to be told twice. I grabbed the ladder and began climbing to the floor above. Reba was on the rungs behind me.

"No, you don't," a voice shouted from below. I stopped and looked back. Reba's left leg was caught in a henchman's grasp. She locked her arm onto the rungs of the ladder and kicked her other leg, smashing her shoe into the man's face. Blood splattered. Another direct hit on the nose. The gigantic man continued to climb and increase his grip on her. She kicked again, this time it was teeth.

"Run!" She looked up at me.

The goon was like a gigantic ape as he climbed up next to Reba and peeled her from the ladder into a hold under his left arm like a sack of potatoes.

I ran up the ladder to the top. I could hear a goon following me. Desperate, I looked around the room. There was a large steel wrench on a wall hook. As I heard the goon huffing up the steps while holding Reba under his arm, I stepped out, took aim, and dropped the metal wrench down the ladder whole. It struck its mark solid. The man's eyes rolled into the back of his head, and he fell directly down the stairs taking Kai with him who was behind him on the stairs and losing his grip on Reba. They landed with a splat.

Fortunately, Reba landed atop the pile. She seemed a bit stunned as she staggered to her feet, stood for a second and shook her head, then started climbing again. I waved at her to hurry when, at that moment, a big hairy arm snatched her from the ladder. Anton wrapped her in a bear hug. "Guess I need you for a bit of insurance, missy." He looked up through the ladder at me. I'll never forget that stare or those cold eyes. I turned and ran.

I reached the street just as an unmarked police car with its blue lights flashing skid to a halt. It was Dad and a detective from San Francisco PD.

"They got Reba..." I told them the short, quick version of what happened. The SF copper called in several units for backup, and we entered the cement plant. I took them to the stairs where the scuffle occurred. The floor showed the outline of the large henchman and the others as it was the only clean spot. We ran into the other room. The scientist, table, lab equipment, and men were all gone. Cleared out. We took the elevator up the next level. This came out in an office and only the plant workers were present. More police units arrived on the scene. "No one left out the gate onto Amador Street," I said. "You guys arrived just as I got out."

"We'll check the back. Sarge, can you keep him safe somewhere?" Dad pointed at me.

I sat in the back of a Ford police vehicle. Reba was a hostage because of me. She was in serious danger and all because of me. Dad's going to hate me. Reba's in lord knows what kind of trouble. Tears welled up, and I began crying. If I wasn't so overconfident about developing the evidence, none of this would've happened.

Almost on queue, two Bell 429 turbo helicopters lifted off from behind the cement plant. One flew north along the bay and the other south and inland, probably heading over the SFO airport. Police radios sparked to life with requests for information on the two helicopters. After they'd disappeared, the dispatcher came back and said that no flight plans had been filed. The door to the police vehicle swung open and a uniformed Lieutenant sat in the driver's seat speaking on his portable radio. "This is a child kidnapping case now, so get onto the Feds and see if those choppers can be tracked."

Dad climbed into the passenger seat.

"Hey, kid," the Lieutenant said looking at me in the rearview mirror. "What more do you know about this?"

"Nothing about the helicopters. You may want to cross reference FAA registrations for any aircraft associated with California International Import and Export, Inc. That's Anton Andropov's company. Most all of the big assets are held in that company's name."

"Thanks, I'm on it." The Lieutenant climbed out of the car leaving Dad and me inside.

The driver's side door opened again and a guy in a basic grey two-piece suit sat in the driver's seat. The back door next to me opened and a fit-looking black man sat next to me. He wore a turtleneck sweater under a tweed sport jacket. I could smell the wool of his jacket.

"Palmer," the man next to me said. "I'm agent Woods, FBI." He flipped open his two-part credentials and let me study them. They looked quite legit. "He's agent Reed," He looked over to my Dad.

"Detective Palmer," Reed said. "Good to see you again."

"JP," Dad said. "Be straight with these guys and tell them what you know."

I went through everything, including Reba and me following Kai into the Redwood lab; Lesta confronting us and lashing us to a lab table with cable ties; watching them steal two vials of the serum; the evidence I captured about the serum; communications to Hong Kong; and the Hong Kong organization insisting on some sort of demonstration.

I pulled out my phone and ran the video that I'd taken before Reba and me were discovered. Pausing on the shot of the scientist, I expanded the still image to his forearm showing the dragon tattoo.

"This is the mark of a Chinese Tong. The Dragon Tong, to be specific," I said.

Agent Reed just stared at the video then back to me.

"Given the equipment set out on the table," I continued. "I think he was going to run some tests on the serum before paying for it and completing the exchange."

"You say that Siri went off before the transaction could be completed?"

I nodded.

"Did you see the vials with the serum?"

"No. Mr. Big just told the Tong scientist that they were crammed into the mouth of a golden dragon sculpture and the other was packed in a briefcase."

"But you didn't see the vials, right?"

"Correct," I said.

"But the two of you saw the vials taken from the Redwood Lab?"

"We were tied up," My voice raised. "Why all the questions? I've told you all of this. Why aren't you going after Reba?"

"That's enough!" Dad looked over his shoulder at the agent in the back of the car with me. "He's not the culprit."

"So, you say," Agent Reed climbed from the car and slammed the doors shut. The other agent left as well.

"I think I know why some of the other detectives call them the Fumbling, Bumbling, Idiots," Dad said.

The radio cracked to life. One of the SFPD units searching along the waterfront side of the plant has found a girl. "She's bruised but okay."

Dad and I jumped from the car and ran along a dirt path to an old wooden wharf behind the plant. A group of officers crowded around a stack of steel barrels by the land side of the Wharf.

"Let me go!" Reba shouted standing and pushing one of the officers away from her. My heart jumped in my chest as I saw here. I ran up and she opened her arms and hugged me. "I got one of the vials," she whispered in my ear.

"This isn't a game, Reba," we separated and looked at one another.

"Yes, it is," She grinned at me. "It's just a bit more physically challenging."

"Rebecca!" Dad ran up and bear-hugged the two of us together. "I thought we lost you."

He set us down.

"I'm not that easily lost," Reba said.

The smart-mouthed Agent Reed pushed between the officers. "I'm Agent Reed," he flashed his two-part FBI credentials. "Mind telling us what happened?"

"Hey," Dad stood between them. "We just found her. Let's get her medically checked out and then chat, okay?"

The agent, knowing Dad was correct, stepped back as a fire/rescue unit rolled onto the dock with its red lights flashing. Two medics jumped out and took Reba to the back of the unit where she sat on the fender while they took vitals and examined her. Dad, Agent Reed, and I stood around them.

"You happy now?" Reed asked Dad.

"I'm better."

"Good," he turned to Reba. "What happened?"

"He threw me out of the Helicopter before they took off," Reba answered.

"How 'bout you start with the moment Siri went off and up to when we found you," Agent Reed was clearly annoyed by her answer.

"Mr. Big grabbed me as JP was able to get away."

"Mr. Big?" He asked.

"Yeah. He's real, real big and strong. Probably a 60-inch chest, arms larger than my legs, and no neck. Named Anton."

She flinched a bit as the blood pressure cuff tightened on her arm. "He grabbed me and flung me under his arm like I was some grain sack. I kicked and punched, but he didn't even notice. His grasp tightened. Felt like he was squeezing the air out of me. Then he carried me through a back tunnel under the cement plant and up onto the wharf area where two helicopters waited."

"And then?" Reed prompted.

"The three Chinese guys got into the first chopper. The one guy still had blue gloves on and a lab coat. As the first chopper's turbines spun up, I could hear sirens approaching. I figured JP got out and found help. At that point, Kai-nam climbed into the second chopper holding a small case and the statue of Fuzanglong. . ."

"Fuzanglong?" Reed interrupted.

I rolled my eyes because I knew what was coming. Reba sparked up and rambled on about the mythical Chinese dragon. At one point, I looked at Dad and his face had that knowing smile that she was actually lecturing the FBI about a dragon.

"Okay, stop!" the Agent interrupted. "Got it. Dragons."

Reba just kept on with her monolog.

"Stop!" Reed silenced her. "I don't really care about the dragon."

"But it's the key to what's going on," Reba said in a bit of shock.

"What happened next?"

"Lesta showed up just as Mr. Big was about to put me in the helicopter."

"Who showed up?"

"Lesta Andropov," Dad spoke. "He's been active in some gang related activity in the South Bay."

Reed nodded and made yet another note in his notepad. I was surprised that he only wrote notes and wasn't recording the discussion. "So," he looked at Reba, "Why do you say the dragon is the key?"

She glanced at me then back to the agent. "It's come up a lot. In the chat with people in Hong Kong, the sculptures at their house, and at the museum. The dragon, the legends, it's the year of the dragon coming up you know, and the three Tong guys all had dragon tattoos. Fuzanglong must have something to do with everything that's going on."

He took a few more notes in silence.

"I couldn't believe Lesta stopped Mr. Big from taking me. He actually intervened with his father and made him release me."

"So, Mr. Big just let you go?"

"Kind of," Reba answered. "He tossed me like a stuffed animal into the back seat of the helicopter. Lesta and him argued and pushed each other. Then, Mr. Big grabbed my legs and hurled me out of the copter onto the far side of the dock. I hit hard, but judo-rolled with my arms tucked, easing the landing. I remember Lesta looking at me and shaking his head. Then, they got into the helicopter and took off."

"Were you able to track the helicopters?" Dad asked.

The agent just looked down, "We will."

"Reba," Dad said, "did you see any markings or numbers on the helicopter?"

She shook her head. "It was really dark and the wind blowing from them as they took off was too much. I had to keep my eyes shut."

Agent Reed took a deep breath. "Right, when she's cleared, you guys head home. Stafford," he looked at Dad, "we'll be in touch in the morning." Reed took out his cell phone and spoke to someone asking for help from the FAA on two choppers that took off from Pier 90 in San Francisco.

The three of us waited on the curb front of the plant as Dad arranged to get a rental car. One of the SF units would take us to collect the car, but we needed to wait until the SF cops finished their work on the scene. "JP, Detective Palmer," Reba said. "I don't have my cell phone."

"It must have fallen from your pocket," Dad said.

I grabbed mine. Reba and I had set a friend's relationship on the Find-My application. "Let's see if it's still active," I said.

The three of us watched on my phone as the map rendered and exposed the location of the cell phone. The phone reported that it was moving swiftly toward the Farallon Islands, about 20 miles west of the Golden Gate Bridge, "It must have slipped out of your pocket when Anton tossed you into the helicopter."

"What the heck are they doing flying out there?" Dad asked. "There're no airports or land beyond the Islands."

"A boat," Reba said. "I remember something. Just before Anton flung me from the helicopter, he yelled at Lesta that they must now go to the Solaris because of these brats. Then he threw me out."

"That's gotta be it. A ship off the coast," Dad said as he grabbed a business card and his phone.

I did a quick search on the Solaris. It's a 400-foot-long yacht. "Wait," I said before Dad finished typing the phone number. "It's a yacht owned by one of the wealthiest Russian oligarchs, last location outside Bodrum, Turkey. Reba, are you sure about the name?"

She thought for a moment. "I think that's what he said. It sure sounded like it."

I pointed at my phone again. "We're assuming that they maintain a westward heading and rendezvous with a ship. I don't know. If they're high-end choppers, they can easily do a range of 400 miles. They may turn inland again."

"Ye of little faith!" Dad frowned at me then tapped to connect his call. "Reed," he barked, dropping the polite title of Agent, "Reba dropped her cell phone into the helicopter. It's just passing over the Farallon Islands on a course due west. We'll lose the signal soon. You may want to ask your counterparts at the D.H.S. for some Coast Guard help."

I shook my head as Dad pocketed his cell phone, "He hung up?"

"Actually, he thanked me, then rang off."

"He didn't ask you for Reba's phone number or anything?"

Dad sighed. The answer was clearly no.

"Guys," Reba added in a sheepish tone. "There's something else."

We looked at her. Dad prompted her to give.

"I may have lost my phone because I snatched this," she held a single, capped vial of green liquid up for us to see.

"Is that what I think it is?" I said.

She nodded, "I probably lost my cell phone when I opened the case that he tossed onto the floor of the helicopter and took this out. There were three vials in separate padded sleeves. Two were clear liquid and this was the only one that looked like green goo."

"He tossed me out of the chopper, and I rolled to protect this."

We stared at the vial as she held it up letting a small bit of light shine through.

A MOLE INSIDE

The next morning, Reba and I were kept out of school on orders of the FBI. I was more concerned that Mum and Dad had stayed home from work, A bit later Mrs. Ng and Reba came over. Reba sat, her head held down, legs together and palms pressed together in her lap. She expressed frustration that she might miss an important soccer game with the school team. She held her hands pressed together in front of her as though in prayer.

Earlier, I'd figured the FBI would want most of the evidence that I'd collected up to this point. I didn't want to give them original material or items from the tap that I'd installed in Lesta's home. I sanitized a hard drive. Then copied and organized the evidence files in chronological order so that they could see the material. In the email and communications folder, I placed several files that I'd extracted from the network captures without giving the full capture or listing the provenance.

Mrs. Ng asked a ton of questions that my father handled as best he could. He made it very clear that neither Reba nor I were in trouble with the FBI. Instead, we were confidential witnesses to a potentially significant crime. She was afraid Reba, and their family might be targeted by bad people or even the government. They might be expelled. I learned that she and her husband were in the US as asylum-seekers from Vietnam. They'd worked hard to integrate in their new home and had traveled through several relocation camps at the end of the war. "We don't mean to be involved in something like this," Mrs. Ng said.

My Mum served her a cup of tea while casting an angry look on me and my Dad, "Mrs. Ng., there's nothing to fear."

"There's everything to fear," she burst into tears and hugged her daughter close as they sat on the sofa. "These bad men may come back at us, and the government made us sign that we wouldn't be involved in any such activity."

"They're witnesses," Dad said. "Confidential witnesses. Nothing more. If anything, they might get a reward."

I don't know where Dad came up with the reward idea.

"The only reward might be a bullet, or we might get sent back."

"No. Nothing like that."

Thank goodness the doorbell rang at this moment. The room fell silent as Mum opened the door.

Agent Reed, dressed in slacks, a white polo shirt and sport coat came in along with a woman dressed in a neat, grey pant suit accompanied by a silky-white blouse. She knows how to dress, I thought. He introduced her as Agent Wilson. Reed sat across from us and Agent Wilson stood holding a tablet PC. Finally, some technology other than a ballpoint pen.

"How's Rebecca this morning?" Reed asked of Mrs. Ng.

"Just bruised. She's fine otherwise. What's going to happen now?"

"I'm sure all of you have questions. We'll get to those in a bit, if we have time," he turned to me. "Jason Palmer, what would you like to share with me that led up to last evening?"

I held up a drive, "This drive contains various digital artifacts and evidence..."

"Ha," Reed said. "What does a 9th grader know about evidence?"

A pin could have dropped in the room and made a thundering noise.

"Quite a lot actually, Agent Reed," I regained my thoughts. "As I was saying, this contains evidence that was acquired when we tripped over several elements."

Reed was about to speak when the woman, Agent Wilson said, "Let's see what this young man has to say."

I smiled. Maybe she was the boss. "The files go back several months and show ongoing criminal activity that started with the kidnapping of a dog."

"A dog?" Reed said.

"Let's hear him out," Wilson said.

"A few students at school were extorting good grades from our math teacher after they stole and held the teacher's dog hostage. Reba, sorry Rebecca and I uncovered digital evidence that led us to a warehouse on Halloween night. While searching for the dog inside the warehouse, we happened to see a transaction taking place involving diamonds in exchange for stolen identities of hundreds of wealthy people."

"We intervened," Dad interrupted, "investigated and made several arrests at the scene. The diamonds recovered were worth a few million and were actually blood diamonds."

"So that case is closed, right?" Reed said. "Jason, can you bring us more current?"

"I just want you to have a foundation and some background, so you understand why we were in a position to obtain the information," I said. "This brings us to our week at science camp, up in the Santa Cruz redwoods." Reba looked up at me, a hint of fear in her eyes. I pressed on, "We observed one of the other students, Kai-nam Andropov sneak away from class and head through the woods."

"How is Kai-nam involved?" Wilson asked in a melodic, polite voice.

"Kai was present last evening at the cement factory."

Wilson showed no emotion but made a note on her tablet. I had Reed's attention.

"We followed him. He went under the fence at the place we now know was a lab in the redwoods. There are photos of him messing with some of the electrical panels. Next, we know that the door access system unlocked, and he went inside. It's now that he and Lesta, his Dad..."

"Lesta Andropov," Dad added.

"Right," I cleared my throat. "It's now that Lesta and Kai connected to a system, removed data, and then stole some vials from one of the refrigeration units."

Reed waved the palm of his hand at me, and Wilson smiled looking at me. Did my eyes move? Did I glance to the right? I pressed on anyway. "On the drive, there were documents about the serum that was stolen and subsequent communications between members of the Andropov family and email addresses in Hong Kong. The reports describe. . ."

"Hold up little fella," Reed said. My Dad almost stood. "You've created more questions than answers for us. You're bright and know something about C.S.I. We need more to understand the provenance of this evidence."

I let out a heavy sigh.

"What Agent Reed means," Agent Wilson started.

"The beginning of something's existence or origin," I finished for Wilson. She smiled and nodded while Reed waved his fingers in a come-here or give me more sign.

"I can mount the drive," I said, "and show you the information we obtained."

"Where did it come from?"

"Stop," Reba stood and took a few steps forward. "The cat needs to come out of the bag, or so they say."

"Reeeba," I called.

"No JP," she said. "They need to know." She turned, looked at her Mum and then at my parents. "JP and I followed Kai, keeping our distance and avoiding detection as he went into the lab. We trailed him deeper into the facility."

"I don't believe there was any security video footage of that," Wilson said.

I shook my head. "The actions Kai took disabled both the CCTV, access control and alarm systems."

"There were no lights on the cameras or movement by them. He completely disabled the system," Reba said.

Reed smirked as Wilson took a few more notes. Now, Reed motioned to Reba. I sat down.

"We followed Kai through several corridors until he came to a glassed-in lab room. On my phone, I took a video of him as he accessed one of the computer stations."

"He plugged in a USB drive," I said. "Typed several commands, waited a bit, then extracted the drive and left the lab. When clear, we went in, and I took a triage image of the system. That shows the times that he obtained the information and which files he moved onto the thumb drive."

"Do you have information on the thumb drive?" Wilson asked.

"Yes. I have the make, model and factory serial number of the thumb drive."

"Thank you. Proceed Ms. Ng."

Reba looked at me and then back to Agent Wilson. "We were about to bail out, when the lab door banged open and Lesta with some big-ass creep barged in. He directed the guy to get us, and he came at me. I threw a fast sidekick and broke his nose."

"Okay," Wilson said. "That explains some of the splattered blood we found in the lab. Please, continue."

Blood, I thought. Great. That would show that someone else was in the lab room and not just us. Yay for squishy biology stuff.

"They rounded us up and used wire wraps to strap JP and me together, then tied us to one of the lab benches." Mrs. Ng pressed a handkerchief to her nose and eyes and let a whimper. Mum changed seats and hugged Mrs. Ng.

"Once we were strapped in tight, Lesta and his man started searching through the refrigerators. They found and took three vials that contained a dark green liquid."

"Reba got us free by getting a pair of scissors to cut our way out," I said.

"That was the wrist injury I treated after picking you up from camp," Mum said. Now tears welled in her eyes.

I nodded.

"You brat," she said. Dad was silent, his arms crossed, and his stare cut through me.

Agent Wilson waved her hand silencing my Mum. "You all can settle this later," Wilson looked at Reba and me. "Go on."

"Not much more to say, really. We gathered ourselves and started to leave the lab when the security systems activated. Cameras came on. Alarms sounded."

"You could have told me!" Dad said.

"When?" I said. "You had fuzzy camera pictures of Reba and me in the lab. You said the FBI lab was working to clear the images. We thought you'd think we were prime suspects."

Mrs. Ng sobbed, even Reba was crying, while Dad just looked away.

"We had to work to clear ourselves," I said. "So, we dug deeper, and that's where we intercepted the communications and all the other information that led us to the museum and cement plant."

"They were meeting to sell the serum to the three Chinese Tong members," Reba said. Mrs. Ng glanced up fear in her face.

"And," Reed said. "How, pray tell, do you know they were members of a Tong?"

"Tattoos on their arms. The photos are on the drive. They're members of a dark, Chinese organization running out of Hong Kong and Macao. They all three had the exact same tattoo on the underside of their right forearms."

Both Reed and Wilson whispered between themselves. Then Reed put his hand out and accepted the drive.

"This is what they were after," Dad stood holding an evidence bag with a single vial of green liquid. "Last night, Reba had the sense and chance to grab one of the vials after

Anton tossed her into the helicopter. She protected it when he threw her out."

"Why didn't you give us this last night?"

Reba stuck her hand up, "Because I'd only met you and I didn't know if I could trust you."

Reed just shook his head.

"You weren't nice. You weren't understanding. You treated me like crap." Oh goodness. Reba was on roll.

I stepped in, "Look, she was in shock last night and gave it to Dad on the way back in the car."

Reed looked directly at my Dad, "You'll be hearing more about this."

I moved to confront Reed.

"Stop. Now." Wilson barked as she slapped her tablet closed. "Agent Reed, I think we have a lot to follow up on. Do we have the warrant?"

"Signed just before we came in."

"Get the team together and let's hit that house."

Reed nodded and made for the door. It's like he couldn't wait to leave. I was glad to see the backside of him as the door closed.

"And," Wilson continued, "You two are very brave and very smart. I want you to stay here and home from school today until I return."

"Yes, ma'am." I said.

Reba saluted.

Mrs. Ng was smiling now. Brave and smart was all she needed to hear. She exclaimed that she'd go home and cook all of us a great lunch. Mum was a different story. She was still upset and stormed out of the room. Dad just shook his head and said, "It's a bit like an old joke. If you ask a rookie what he'd do if he had to arrest his mother. He says, 'call for backup.'" Dad left the room after her.

Reba and I were the only two left in the room. "Come on," I motioned toward my room. Leaving the door open and lights on, I logged into my tap. "I discovered something new. I can remotely connect to their home surveillance system."

The computer screen tiled eight cameras across the screen. We had a view of the front drive, the inside of the front door, and a few sides of the house. Just not the side Reba and I approached it on that night.

Three vehicles stopped outside the gate and Agent Reed talked into an intercom.

"Hold on," I tapped commands into the video system which also had the intercom. Agent Reed's voice cracked and fuzzed like any intercom.

"FBI. We have a search warrant and will crash these gates down unless you open them now!" Reed was definitely hot under the collar.

"Again," Reed repeated his notice.

"I think I'll help him out," I said. I sent a signal across the home network that I'd seen dispatched to the access control system. Sure enough, the gates swung back.

Moments later, four unmarked cars and two San Jose uniformed units swarmed in toward the drive and front door. The big Korean with the recently healed nose opened the door to the pounding fists and the FBI grabbed and cuffed him.

They sat him on a bench just outside the entrance and left a San Jose copper to guard him.

"There're not many cameras inside the house," I said. "So, we can't see what they're actually doing."

"This is entertaining," Reba said. "But you and I both know that no one of significance is actually there."

"Yeah, but it sure feels good." I tapped a few more commands into a shell. "I'm going to dump one more packet capture from the system. I'm guessing that they'll take everything and shut down the network and all communications into and out of the house."

"Yeah, I wonder," Reba pondered. "Do you think Agent Reed knows what a computer looks like, much less a network?"

"Wilson does," I glanced back at Reba. "He seems more like a smash-it gorilla than someone with skill and tact. He'll just smash everything he doesn't understand." Alt-F5 and the Mario jingle played on my speakers.

"Yup. A real DK."

We laughed.

#

It was dinner time. The Ng and Palmer family sat at the dining table at Reba's home. CaCee, was the only one missing. She went out with friends for a burger and shake.

Dad's cell phone rang, and he left the room to answer the call.

"Well, maybe we toast the Siege of Gibraltar," Dad smiled returning to the table.

The Ng's looked quizzically at him, and Reba smiled. "So, there's a silver lining to this whole matter?"

"Yes, there is. The US Attorney assigned to this case has just granted confidential informant status to both of you." He pointed to Reba and me.

"I don't understand," Mrs. Ng said.

"That means that both of the kids are protected by the US Government. Their identities and information they provided will be protected from disclosure."

She frowned.

"It means the kids are safe," Mum said, raising her glass of juice in a toast.

"Agent Wilson said that they discovered a bunch of evidence that's all going back to the lab."

"Wait," I said. This was actually most troubling. "They sent evidence back to the lab in Quantico?"

"They have other labs. There's one in San Mateo County."

I shook my head. Enough said at this gathering. I got stuck into the large bowl of broth, meats and vegetables. The heat made my nose run. Dad squirted a bunch of hot sauce in his and turned beet red on his first slurp. He sat back waving his hand in front of his mouth, and Mum asked for a glass of milk, which he swallowed in a single gulp.

"Wow!" Dad wiped the sweat from his brow, then the whole napkin rubbed over his face.

Mrs. Ng smiled, "Bobo, mi chang."

Reba laughed, "Naive white guy."

Everyone laughed, and Dad contorted a face while breathing deeply.

"You okay, honey?" Mum inquired, frowning at him. "He always has to be the center of attention."

I just watched thinking about the evidence on the disk I gave the FBI. They claim to have found evidence in the home as a result of the search. I wondered if they even looked at my drive.

After dinner and a wonderful, sweet dessert, Mrs. Ng wanted to play bridge. Reba's Mum and Dad sat at a card table across from my parents. Reba and I went to the far side of the room looking at my cell phone. I scanned to see if I could locate Reba's phone again, and the screen remained blank.

"No sign of my phone?" Reba asked looking over my shoulder at my screen.

I shook my head.

Dad was the "dummy" in the game and stood from the table. His cell phone rang at that moment, and he left the room to answer. In a few moments, he came back and walked over to Reba and me.

"Work just assigned me as liaison to the FBI."

"That's good, right?" I asked.

"Well, it's light duty if you would. They've reassigned all my cases to other detectives." He sighed. "They've put me on a shelf."

"There's got to be a silver lining."

"Only if we bust this case open big. Otherwise, I'm probably heading for parking detail." Dad returned to his seat at the table.

"We're going to check out some stuff on my computer and play a game," I announced. Reba and I left for my house and room. I wanted to check the network traffic one more time.

In my room, I logged into the tap that was still operating inside Lesta and Kai's house. "I'm a bit surprised they didn't take out all the network equipment."

"Maybe the FBI added their own tap?"

"I'll check." Once I connected, I ran a quick NMAP scan to detect hosts across the network. Several of the computers were gone from the network, but all the cameras and communications equipment were still there and operating. As the network data was downloading, I went into my closet and examined the family tree I'd made. There must be something here that I'm missing.

Reba used another machine and printed out the pictures we'd taken at the cement plant that clearly showed the two Tong members and the scientist. In one picture, the scientist held the vial up to a light and examined the contents. He was about to put it into a plastic, sealed examination chamber when Siri proclaimed our presence, disturbing the whole transaction.

I pasted the photos on the wall and connected lines back to the wrestling picture of big Anton. "They didn't finish the deal and must be planning to meet again." Reba said watching me attach the lines.

"But where and when?"

Reba nodded. "Then there's the helicopter. It flew directly out over the Pacific. My phone hasn't been back online since they flew into international waters."

"Good point." I pulled up the specs on the Bell 429 helicopter and printed that out, then attached that picture to the same wall. "Depending on the weight on board, the chopper had about a 400 nautical-mile range." Using Google maps, I plotted the location of the cement plant and drew an arc at 400 miles. "If they kept flying on this course, they would have to encounter a ship that they could land on."

"Aircraft carrier?" Reba asked.

"I doubt it. I don't think Anton would have that kind of money. Now, a high-end yacht, maybe. Remember the last thing you said Anton mentioned before tossing you out of the helicopter?"

"Solaris?"

"Yup." I searched for Solaris on the computer. I found references to some Soviet science fiction drama from 1972 and a remake of the film in 2002.

"Add the word ship and see what you get."

I typed the word ship in front of Solaris and came up with a 140-meter-long yacht owned by one of the Russian oligarchs and flagged out of the Cayman Islands. Vessel Finder showed the yacht moored in Bodrum, Turkey 40-days ago. An overview of the yacht showed a very convenient helipad on the upper stern deck. I printed out another picture that would be hung on my wall. "The location is old and over a 40-day period. It could have sailed into the Pacific by now."

"They'd cross through the Suez Canal and through the Indian Ocean. Doesn't the Canal keep records of ship crossings?"

Good point. I typed several queries and went to the Suez Canal Authority site. There were no records related to ship crossings. According to the site, the records were considered confidential for security reasons. "So, this is a possibility," I looked at Reba. "If this is correct, and we have no real proof that it is, then this whole case could be much bigger than we first thought." The theory was plausible. Without the tail number of the helicopter, we couldn't look up any flight plans or even tell if the chopper didn't fly in a 200-mile arc and land back in the States. Then again, if it did, we'd probably get a signal back from Reba's phone.

"Okay," Reba said. "Let's assume they landed on a ship that was nearly 200-miles out in the Pacific. What then? They're on a boat. The Tong guys flew off somewhere else. Most likely not the same boat."

"Agreed. Maybe this network traffic will tell us something," I opened the packet capture file using my filter script and then ran Zeek. There was a fair amount of email traffic coming through the VPN connection and routed out to the network. Clearly, someone was logging in through the VPN and posting emails.

Zeek logs first. Not my usual, but the presence of the email traffic made me think about the logs. The connection log showed several connections from a new IP address and connections going out to the IP in Hong Kong. This caught my eye, and I altered the analysis script to correlate the email traffic. Interesting that the traffic was destined for a server I hadn't seen before. "Reba, use the other computer and open up the NMAP file dated today."

She knew right where to look on my server's share for the file. "Got it."

"Do you have a machine numbered 10.50.0.222?"

"Yup. OS detection says Linux. Ports 25, 80, 465, and 587 are open. Everything else is filtered or closed."

"It looks like they've got a secondary mail transport server," I entered a couple more commands. "The primary mail server must have been taken by the FBI in the search. This traffic is connecting to port 587 so I can't read the traffic from the network packet capture."

Reba stood and came over to the machine I was working on and looked over my shoulder. "What now?"

"Let's see if we can find this device and other traffic to it. Did the NMAP have the MAC address of the network interface card?"

Reba looked back and got the MAC. The first three hex digits were: D8, 3A, DD. I Googled these digits, and it came back as being a default set by Raspberry Pi, Ltd. I should have guessed. Somewhere, hidden, was a tiny, single board Linux computer no larger than a deck of cards. Hardwired or wireless, this device could be easily concealed. Adding a flash memory card to it would give the system enough room to easily store and manage emails.

I entered it into the Zeek logs and found a bunch of traffic, including a wake-on-LAN message from several hours ago. If the system was asleep, this message would cause the device to wake up. It also explained why my prior NMAP scans never detected it.

"What is it?" Reba asked.

"Looks like a nice, little Raspberry Pi device. If it was connected to the network and asleep, the FBI would not see it on the network unless they did a low-level ARP scan. That's also why we didn't find it. So, look at these three connection lines in the output." I pointed to the listing on the screen for Reba. "These are wake-on-LAN magic packets sent to that device. If you now look a bit later, these packets going to the firewall are probably a DHCP hello."

"DHCP?"

"Dynamic host configuration protocol. It's how a computer gets an IP address on the local network."

To verify this, I opened a shell onto my tap and sent a DNS request on the IP address to the firewall and it returned the name of mail2. "The box is named mail2. If Lesta or Kai's laptops and mail clients are set to send mail to the primary server and it's offline, they must failover to connect to mail2. Nice."

Reba gave a thumbs up. "But how do we see what they're sending if the traffic is encrypted?"

"Before we brute force our way in, let me run CapLoader and Network Miner on the capture and see if there's an easier way in."

CapLoader ingested the file in a few minutes and displayed all of the network flows. I filtered on machine MAC addresses, since a lot of the interesting inbound traffic may have happened before the IP address was established. The listing showed the wake-up messages. This was followed by 'mail2' identifying itself to the network. The next message was a CURL command followed by another CURL command, and then port 587 traffic was established. "You said port 80 was one of the open ports, right?"

"Yup," Reba said.

"I'm going to extract all of the packets that were involved mail2's port 80 traffic and send them to Network Miner." Two simple clicks and Network Miner parsed the large packet capture file.

"Look!" Reba pointed at one of the tabs. "It says there are passwords."

"Don't get your hopes up." I clicked and sure enough. "You're right. There is a single clear text password. That's rare. Then again, they're not using SSH to remotely manage this thing." I copied down the password and opened a terminal screen on my tap. I then typed a 'curl' command to connect to the Web server on port 80. I was prompted only for a password, which I provided. Another terminal screen opened and displayed a list of actions as a menu.

"OMG!" I said. "It's a Web Shell. Just like the type a hacker would install as a back door on a system."

Reba looked at the screen and then at me.

"These are tiny Web sites that are embedded usually by bad guys when they hack into a system."

"So, they hacked their own machine?"

"Naw. They're just using a tool that would have been embedded onto a victim site. They're small and have a bunch of functionalities." This Web shell produced a text-based screen that could easily be loaded into a terminal. One of the options was to run a Start command, probably how they booted up the mail server. The other was to open a superuser command prompt. I selected that, and the terminal screen showed a prompt with a pound sign. I was root. Now it's time to extract the mailbox. I made certain that there was enough room on my tap, then confirmed the location of the mailbox file in /var/spool as well as the location of all mail attachments under the user's home folder.

"What are you doing now?" Reba asked.

"I'm checking out both the physical and logical structures of the file system." I typed 'fdisk -l'. A single physical device was listed as /dev/sda and three logical partitions, sda0, sda1 and sda2. The root folder and boot partition were assigned to /dev/sda0. Interestingly, /home was assigned to /dev/sda1 and /var/spool assigned to /dev/sda2. Whoever built this Raspberry Pi system had a bit of fun isolating the home and spool folders onto separate logical partitions. This may have been done to facilitate backup synchronization or some other cloud mail synch capabilities. In the end, it made my job easier since all I needed was on sda1 and sda2.

"The three logical partitions are very convenient," I said. "Now I remotely image them and store the images on my tap. Then, I'll download them so we can analyze what's been happening."

On my tap, I created a folder called /home/raspberryMail then started Netcat to listen on port 22401 and pipe the output to a 'dd of=/home/raspberryMail/sda0.img'. Then, on the Raspberry Pi system, I typed: 'dd if=/dev/sda0 bs=64M | nc 10.10.50.5 22401'. This ran like a champ. Since it was passing 64-meg chunks across a local connection, no need for compression as speed was just not a problem.

"This is where a confidential forensic investigation crosses into the realm of black-hat hacking," I said to Reba. She frowned. "I'm doing the same thing a hacker would do to extract data from a system, except I'm collecting a forensically sound image of this mail system. Let me queue the other two logical partition extracts to start after this and we'll head back for some dessert and see what the parents are up to. In an hour or so, we should have what we need."

On the walk back, Reba asked a ton of questions about why Lesta and Kai would set up such a system in their house. Simple. It's a bit of a failsafe in case their primary mail server went down. "Clearly, one of the systems the FBI took to their lab was the primary mail server. Ha, ha," I stopped walking just in front of her door. "This would explain why the partitions were configured the way they were. They probably replicated using rsync or something like that into the partitions. I'll bet money on the fact that they had a routine set to destroy the partitions if someone tampered or took the systems out of the rack."

"Really, so if the FBI found the primary mail server and disconnected it, they'd remove files. How can that be?"

"Kai's smarter than that," I said. "Standard forensic response practice is to collect a triage image or full forensic image from a live system before you shut it down. Since it's a Linux box, they probably left it logged in without a password on the console screen as a temptation. If someone mounted a USB drive and then ran a collection tool like dd, or dcfldd, this would trigger an action to destroy the /var/spool/mail folder and the /home user folders with the attachments while the dd or dcfldd tools were running over the root partition first."

"So, even though they took the mail server, the FBI may have nothing?"

"Yup. All was sync'd to the Raspberry Pi system. Let's just hope there's not a similar anti-forensic program in place on this." I shook my head and looked back at my house.

"What's up?"

"I'm just so stupid. There could have been a similar tripwire in this Raspberry Pi system, but I already started the dd tool running. I should have dumped memory first, analyzed that, and then ran the dd dumps. I'm so stupid sometimes." I slapped my forehead.

"No, you're not." Reba stepped over to me, wrapping her arms and giving me a hug.

"You don't understand." I pulled back. "As soon as I hit 'enter' on the keyboard, that system may have alerted Kai or the others that I was dumping it, and they could be activating countermeasures now!"

"So, what do you want to do?" Reba still held her arms around me. I could smell her nice lavender scent. No, no, no. Don't get distracted, I told myself.

"Anyone who goes to the trouble to hide a Pi and isolate /var/spool and /home into separate partitions, has an alarm and detection strategy," I leant forward and buried my head into her shoulder. She patted my back.

"JP, you'll do what you can. You've kept us out of trouble. Now, let's see what you get."

"You're right." No use crying about spilt milk. It won't roll back time. All we can do is wait and see. She gave me a little kiss on the cheek, and we walked on. She kissed me! I blushed red hot. I'm more than alright.

#

It was a few minutes after nine-thirty when Reba and I returned to my computers. The parents were playing their third game of bridge as we headed back to my house.

The system had concluded the extraction of the partitions and there were three compressed image files on my tap. I initiated a download and extracted the files to my laptop. I marked a drive as the original and then copied files to another drive that I marked as working. Then, I fired up Autopsy and loaded the raw image files as data sources from the Raspberry. At the same time, I ran four ingest modules against the volumes: hash lookup with the latest Linux NSRL, file type identification, embedded file extractor and email parser. That should be enough.

"Well," I said, "we got the partitions at least. Ingests are running. If they had a program that was going to destroy contents, it may have run. We'll know in a bit if we get rubbish in Autopsy."

"Wow!" Reba exclaimed pointing at the Autopsy screen. "386 emails already after processing only 20% of the files and 27 communication accounts."

"Yup. Those 27 actually represent relationships where email or messages were actually exchanged," I said proudly. "In a bit, we'll use the communications visualizer to examine those relationships."

Once Autopsy had processed over half of the image files, I opened the viewer. It presented all of the communications.

Ding. Ding.

My cell woke up and popped a message from Dad. I read it and showed my phone to Reba. "Dads got to go to the jail and book the henchman with the busted nose into custody for the FBI."

"I guess that's good," Reba said.

I kept running through the email threads. There was one from a few hours ago that was routed to an account called "man_1". It included text that read like a postcard and an attachment that I opened. It was a photo of the Fuzanglong sculpture that we saw at the cement plant except this one was set on a red leather couch and photographed. "That's interesting. A stupid email that says they're having a wonderful time and sending him a photo."

"Code?" Reba asked.

"I don't know. I need to run a picture analyzer in Autopsy to see if there's anything else of interest hiding in the photo."

Reba headed home for the night at this point. Her parents would be wanting her to get to bed at a reasonable time. That said, we were still under direct FBI instructions not to attend school tomorrow either. I hung and watched the little blue status bar creep across the screen as the ingest module did its job. Not too long now. It finished.

There was one message dispatched to the mail server in Hong Kong, an email account I'd intercepted previously. Clearly from Mr. Big, this message expressed frustration that one of the vials had been lost. The vitriolic response threatened to cut the transaction value in half for Anton's bungling. He could only redeem himself if he obtained and delivered the whole laptop from the Redwood Lab and if the demonstration was successful. To get the whole laptop, they'd have to break in again and that would be very risky, I thought. The security systems at the lab had to be getting refreshed and a 24-hour guard may even be on-site after the prior incident. I was real surprised when a message from Anton some two hours later claimed that obtaining the laptop wouldn't be a problem and that it would be delivered at their next meeting. No mention anywhere about the time and location for the next meeting.

I opened the EXIF analysis file that Autopsy created while running the photo analyzer. Thumb Cache output from the analysis identified three separate photos of Fuzanglong. Each the same snapshot of the dragon statue resting on the couch. On the surface, the photos were identical and had been discovered associated with mail messages in Kai's user directory. Anton using his grandson's technical skills for sure. The one noticeable fact was that all three images were of different file sizes. Two were larger in size than the smallest of the three.

Looking back to the communication viewer, I discovered that one message went from Anton to man_1, possibly the big goon with the busted nose, who had a mail account on the Raspberry system. The other went to a random 25-character mail account name string at Gorilla mail, an anonymous mail service.

I was getting way too tired to focus on these two emails, so I changed and fell fast asleep.

#

The next morning, Reba came over way too early and woke me up. Mum had gone to work, and Dad was fast asleep on the sofa, snoring away. He'd left the front door unlocked so Reba just wandered in.

I staggered off to the shower with a handful of clothes from a drawer. The hot water was invigorating, and I felt alive and ready to go again.

As I stepped back into my room, Reba said, "I was looking at your screen. Did you notice that there is a slight size difference between the images sent to the Gorilla mail account and the other to man_1?"

"Really?"

She nodded, "Just a few bytes, but they're different."

I stared at the screen hoping I'd be fully awake soon.

"Math is sort of my thing," Reba added.

I nodded and dragged both images into a graphical differencer that would compare the bytes between the two files. All was the same except each had a different string of characters embedded near the end of file markers and after the end of the image. Extracting the 111-byte string sent to Gorilla mail, I popped it into a converter. It read, "Du hast morgen um 10 Uhr einen Spa-Termin. Laptop im unverschlossenen Auto lassen." German.

"A spa appointment?" Reba said. "My German isn't that good."

"There's always Google translate." After a quick cut and paste and then read aloud, "You have a spa appointment tomorrow at 10 a.m. Leave your laptop in the unlocked car."

Reba and I looked at each other. I performed the same action with the 119-byte string from the other photograph sent to Man_1.

"Go figure," I said. "It's Korean and reads: Get laptop by Saratoga spa from car and drop to place 77."

"The laptop!"

"Yup. Looks like Mr. Big has a mole inside the lab and they're arranging to steal the laptop. That's how he's going to get it to the drop off. We need to get Dad up."

Reba ran to the other room and worked to rouse my Dad. I had one more thing to check. Back on Autopsy, I opened the EXIF analysis folder, then highlighted the three images of the Fuzanglong dragon. They'd been taken by an iPhone and both had the same geo-coordinates: 33.6088665,-142.2078896. Pasted into Google maps, this translated to 33°36'31.9"N 142°11'22.1"W, a point in the middle of the North Pacific Ocean. Our thought that the helicopter landed on a ship was absolutely correct.

Once again, I checked the location of Solaris and it was still reported moored in Turkey, halfway around the world. Maybe the name Solaris was some sort of code as well.

AN AGITATED STAKEOUT

Dad scrambled quickly when Reba told him what we had discovered. "Lesta's goon will be released by 9AM this morning," he rubbed his eyes. "That's just 20 minutes from now. Assuming he gets his phone back and walks out of the jail, he'll be on the road within an hour."

Dad reappeared after washing his face and grabbing a coat, "JP, grab your stuff. You and Reba are coming along on this one. Might need your tech skills. But you two have to promise not to do anything crazy."

We agreed. Nothing crazy. Just watch and report.

I packed my backpack with the silver drone, a lightweight laptop, my tablet, and a handful of trackers. Reba ran over to her parents and came back in jeans, trainers, dark sweater, and a pair of sunglasses.

"Really?" I barked seeing her. "Sunglasses?"

"You get your techy stuff, and I'll get my stuff." She had a small tote with her and pulled a blonde wig from the bag. "It's CaCee's. She won't miss it."

"Let's go!" Dad shouted already halfway out the door.

#

We headed out and parked a short distance from the jail's release door. Dad called in and asked to be notified when Lesta's henchman was out-processed. Ding. Only a few minutes passed when Dad got the message that the subject had finished. The door swung open and a large Korean with a broad chest and flattop hair stepped out. It was one of those frequent stormy days in San Jose and a light rain started to fall. Our target moved quickly to the street corner and climbed into one of the many taxis that waited in line outside the jail for the releases.

Dad kept a safe following distance behind the taxi. Sure enough, he headed on the 20 or so minute drive back to Pinnacle community. The cab cleared the checkpoint. Dad showed his police ID, and we followed. Lesta's house was the last on the cul-de-sac. The whole neighborhood looked different in the light. Houses sparkled even though a light rain fell, and the street was freshly washed. Dad positioned the undercover car down a bit from the entrance so we could watch.

"Shall I put the drone up so we can have a bird's eye view of activity inside the gates?"

"You can fly in this rain?" Dad said.

I dug the grey drone from my pack and began opening the four propellers. "It shouldn't be too much of a problem. Give me a minute and we should have our eyes in the sky."

"No need," Reba said pointing at the intersection. "That's the black Lincoln Town Car."

The Korean drove out onto the street, not noticing our grey Ford Taurus parked a few hundred feet away. Engine and lights off. Not even the windshield wipers on.

"Good catch, Reba," Dad said as he started the engine, and we pulled out slowly. A white sedan was between us and the Town Car. The henchman swung left at Blossom Hill Road, and we followed.

"Wish I had the drone up," I said.

"Can you do it from a moving car?"

"Nope."

"Well," Dad said. "Then we have to do this the old-fashioned way. And hope we don't lose him, or he doesn't burn us."

Again, we followed on a route through several communities and two-lane roads. It rained harder now, and visibility degraded as the water fell, making it difficult to follow the black car at a safe distance. At one traffic light near Los Gatos, we actually pulled up behind the Town Car. Reba and I ducked, her lying across the back seat and me curled up looking at my shoelaces.

"He's moving," Dad said.

"That was close," Reba commented as we sat up. "Where's he going?"

"Wherever it is, it's got to be close by," Dad remarked. "Otherwise, why wouldn't he have taken the motorway."

"Could he be heading back to the lab?" She asked.

"Maybe, but he's alone. I don't think he'd risk going there by himself."

"But that's just a few miles away."

The car came onto Big Basin Way at the entrance to the rustic high street of Saratoga. Cars lined both sides of the street parked in front of shops and cafes. The sidewalk tables and chairs were empty but inside, the restaurants were jammed with breakfast diners. I felt hungry. This had all happened too quick, and I didn't get to pack any emergency food in my backpack. Maybe we could grab something quick from one of the coffee places. The car turned into a wide alleyway that led to a motor hotel entrance that had half a dozen empty parking spaces. The alley separated a day spa on one side and a bric-a-brac shop on the other. The Town Car parked in the last space. Dad pulled a quick left turn onto a cross street and parked in front of a fire hydrant. Reba kept watch out the back window. "He's getting out of the car," Reba alerted.

"Great," Dad said. "In the rain no less."

"He's walking toward us and just turned right heading down the sidewalk in front of the spa."

"You two, stay here and watch the car. Don't get into trouble." Dad stepped out and moved along the sidewalk, then disappeared down the street.

"Let's get a tracker onto that Town Car," I pulled a small magnetic box from my bag.

Reba grabbed it from my hand. She'd pulled on a black rain slicker with a hood. "My job, not yours."

She was out of the car before I could protest. I couldn't believe how casual she walked across the main street and down the alley. As she passed the back of the Town Car, she bent down for a second and secured the tracker to the car's gas tank. Then, just as casually, waltzed back after waiting for a couple cars to pass.

"I couldn't see your Dad anywhere as I crossed the street," She said shutting the car door behind her.

I had my tablet pad out and communicated with the tracker. It worked perfectly.

A couple of minutes went by, and a red Mini Cooper turned into the alleyway and backed into a space near the middle of the parking area. A lady, wearing a gray trench coat, climbed out and popped open an umbrella. Reba opened her side window, reaching out with her phone to snap pictures. The woman held a clutch briefcase in one hand and the umbrella in another. She looked around, stepped over to the Town Car and, juggling the umbrella and the briefcase with one hand as she popped open the Town Car's backdoor. We watched her slap the door shut, straighten herself, and then avoid growing puddles as she walked toward the main street holding only the umbrella and a small purse.

"She's dropped the briefcase into the back of the Town Car. It's a dead drop," I dug inside my pack and pulled out a credit card sized sleeve and activated a tracker that acknowledged with a chirp. "We need to get this in that briefcase."

"Give it to me," Reba snatched the tracker from me.

The woman turned the corner and went into the day spa.

Reba slipped on the blonde wig and kept her hood down so the long blond locks flowed over her shoulders. She was out of the car and sauntering back toward the alley again. This time she had to wait for several cars to pass on the main street before crossing. She moved quickly as though dodging around the heavy rain drops pelting her head. She was in the alley way and popped open the back seat door of the Town Car. This time it took her a bit to fumble with the briefcase and get clear. All the while, my heart raced. I really hoped the big goon wouldn't walk back. "Come on, Reba. Get out of there," I said aloud to myself.

The Town Car's door shut, and Reba stepped clear. My first relief. She pulled the hood of her slicker and tucked in the golden wig locks in the hoody as she approached the crossing back toward us. After a car passed, she walked across the street, her head down and face concealed. As though on queue, the goon appeared walking briskly toward his Town Car. That was too close. Once across the street, Reba continued at her normal pace until she climbed into the back of the undercover car.

"That was super close," I said.

"No, that was just awesome. I was super cool and got the tracker planted on the backside of the laptop."

"You can't be serious. Weren't you afraid."

"Fears for losers," she slipped off the wig and slicker. "It's just like striking at soccer. If you're afraid you'll get hurt, then you get hurt. Same thing here. If I panic or am super nervous, then I get caught out."

"Damn, girl," I tapped at my tablet PC. Both trackers reported in, had full battery life, and strong signals. "You did good!"

Dad plopped back into the car as the Korean pulled from the parking space and drove back out the way he drove in on Big Basin Way. "Buckle up. We gotta go."

"Chill, Dad. We've got trackers on the Town Car and on the laptop."

"Wait! What?"

Reba boisterously explained what happened.

"So, we don't have to rush," I added. "He's heading down Saratoga Avenue. Maybe toward the motorway."

"I told you guys not to get out of the car. Damn. You could have been caught or hurt," Dad let out a long sigh and started the engine. "Maybe it's not worth it and I should take you guys home."

"It's worth a whole lot more, detective Palmer," Reba said. "Something really wicked is about to happen and lives may be at stake."

Dad pulled the car back onto Saratoga Avenue and followed my guidance. We were just about a mile behind the Town Car and laptop. Dad stepped on it to close the gap with the Town Car. As he passed through an intersection, a County Sheriff's unit pulled out, switching on the blues and twos. Dad pulled over just before the motorway on ramp. I focused on my map, watching the Town Car's tracker moving down the motorway.

The deputy walked up to the driver's side window. Dad had his badge and ID out.

"Know how fast you were going?" The deputy asked, leaning into the driver's window.

Dad flashed his badge. "Unfortunately, yes." Dad said, holding the badge and credentials low. "On official business."

"With two kids in the car?"

"Yup. Trying to catch up with a suspect. Need them to identify the guy."

"You know, it's wet and I don't want to have to take a crash report on you. But okay. Try not to go more than 10 miles an hour over the speed limit."

He didn't need to tell Dad anything more. "Have a nice day," Dad said as he drove carefully up onto the motorway. "That's just what we needed."

"Looks like Lesta's man is taking the interchange heading north on Highway 17," I said.

"Great. Now we're like three miles behind," Dad said.

"Both trackers are working great. I've still got him," I said.

Dad weaved past a few cars and stepped on the gas. "I'm just at ten over the speed limit."

"Looks more like twenty," Reba smirked looking over from the back seat.

"Not helping."

The tracker showed the Town Car and laptop were still together and traveling north. We rolled on the ramp to highway 17 and again weaved through traffic. "At least I'm back in my jurisdiction now. That Sheriff's unit probably called in my plate. Hopefully, dispatch is busy and didn't take note of the stop. Otherwise, I'm probably in a bit more trouble." He held two hands firmly at nine and three on the car's wheel and continued to press past cars on the freeway.

"Dad, looks like he's taking the Coleman off ramp," I noted.

"Let me know which way he goes on Coleman."

A few moments later, the marker from the tracker turned right and started back over the motorway. "He's heading west up Coleman. Toward the airport."

"Damn, we can't lose him now," Dad pressed the gas pedal harder. Reba slid back into her seat, and the tablet almost slid from my hand. "There's the Coleman exit. Hang on!" Dad swung the car hard into the cloverleaf. The tires squealed even on the wet ramp, their objection to the sharp turn. The rain was coming down hard now and the wipers streaked across the windshield.

"He's on Airport Way heading toward Terminal B," I looked at Dad. His knuckles were white, gripping the steering wheel. "You can back down. Don't get us pulled over again. I've got him."

He breathed deeply and relaxed. Our speed dropped significantly, and we stopped passing other cars.

"He's pulling into the short-term parking lot, just passed the baggage claim area."

Dad cruised slowly past the front of Terminal B. "You two duck down in case he's walking out front," Dad ordered.

"He's stopped and both trackers are at the car. Looks like a parking space closest to the terminal."

Dad navigated up to one of the gates and took the ticket to open the arm. He pulled in and turned to the back of the parking lot. Fortunately, there was a space in the second to last row and he pulled the car nose in.

"Laptops on the move," I said.

"Where?"

"Heading toward the terminal."

"You two, stay here," Dad opened his door and swung his leg out of the car.

"No," I said. "You have no way of tracking the laptop without us."

He paused, "Fine, but stay behind me."

The rain hadn't let up and was falling hard, so we all ran for cover just outside the terminal building. Crowds of arriving passengers stood in the shelter nearest the terminal waiting for pickups.

"Where is he now?"

"Inside, heading toward the ticket counters."

We followed on foot, passing by the four baggage carousels. There's art exhibits and glass cases all around the center of the terminal by the information counter. It's directly beneath the upper platform where departing passengers head for the security checkpoint.

"Wait! Stop!" I looked at my pad with Dad on the left and Reba next to me. "He's turned just short of reaching the ticket counters, probably toward the men's toilet."

We took up a position leaning against a wall. Dad could see the bathroom entrance, while Reba and me were behind. "There, he's coming out now," Dad turned a bit to hide himself. The big goon walked by and continued back toward the baggage carousels. "Okay. Let's go."

"No! The tracker hasn't moved. It's still in the toilet."

"Are you certain?"

I showed him my tablet. The tracker's signal was only a hundred yards away from us, while the big lummox was walking empty-handed toward an exit.

"Could he have found it and tossed the tracker in the rubbish?"

"We best check," Reba said.

I nodded and passed her my tablet and backpack.

"Where are you going?" Dad asked.

"I need to pee," I walked quickly to the restroom. Nobody would suspect a kid going to the bathroom.

Inside, a young Asian man washed his hands. The bag containing the laptop rest on its side on the counter next to him. I walked over to pee, which I really needed to do for some time. As the man tossed his used paper towel, grabbed the laptop bag and headed out carrying the clutch bag with the laptop.

I finished, washed quickly, then went to meetup with Reba and Dad.

"Tag's moving," Reba said.

"No doubt," I said. "He came out just ahead of me. Asian male. Slender. About 30-years old, neatly trimmed black hair and wearing a sleek, black jogging suit."

"Looks like the tag is going up the escalator toward the security checkpoint," Reba passed the tablet back to me.

Dad looked at Reba, "What the hell is your mum going to say now that I've dragged you out here?"

"Not much," she waved her cell phone as we walked off toward the base of the escalator. "I sent her a few texts while in the car letting her know we were in pursuit, and I was with you. She said to be safe and follow your instructions."

The checkpoint wasn't too busy with only a handful of people departing on mid-morning, mid-week flights. "Come on, let's beat 'em through," Dad said.

He walked through the Known Crewmember line, and we followed. At the checkpoint, he showed his badge, stating that this was official business, and the two kids were with him. The security officer made notes on his system including photos of us and snapshot of Dad's credentials, then the officer waited for a response from his computer. Ding. "You're good to go."

Inside, we stood along the main concourse. Reba and I took a position just outside the exit from the security checkpoint and Dad stood across from it. We didn't have to wait long as an Asian woman pushing a stroller accompanied the man I saw in the bathroom. I kept my head buried in my tablet PC while Reba watched. The tracker passed right in front of us. Reba stepped out and followed behind the couple. Dad's eyes widened and he smirked at me, seeing her move. We followed.

"I can't wait until I have to write this all up. Let's just hope that something big happens and we get the collar, otherwise your Mum will kill me when I get fired for this."

The Asian family took seats facing the tarmac closest to the jetway door for a pending outbound Honolulu flight. We sat in a row behind them where we had a clear view should they move. At one point, the Mum got up and pushed the stroller over to the ticket counter. I saw that the tracker moved with her. Probably in the stroller since she wasn't carrying anything. The man just sat staring out the window as the incoming jet parked at the gate. The flight was scheduled to depart in an hour. The woman stopped at the ticket counter and obtained a gate-check tag for the baby stroller, then rolled back to sit with her partner. The baby started crying and the Mum took the kid out of the stroller and began feeding it with a bottle.

"Now what?" I asked Dad.

"You two sit here and keep an eye on them. I'm going to check in with Agent Wilson."

Dad left and disappeared somewhere on the concourse. Nothing much happened for the few minutes he was gone.

"We can't really let them board the plane," Reba said.

I shook my head, "We may have no other choice. They're clearly transporting the laptop and it's kind of our only lead."

Dad returned but didn't come and sit with us. Instead, he stepped up to the gate ticket counter. I saw that he showed his badge and had a silent word with the airline agent. Next, he pulled out what looked like a credit card. After a few minutes, he walked over and sat with us.

"Well?" I asked. Reba looked at him too.

"Reba," Dad said. "You're sure that your Mum said it was okay for you to be here with me?"

"Yup. Look at my phone and the text thread." She held her mobile phone so he could see the screen.

"Let me call her." Dad got up again and disappeared. A moment later he returned. "Did they do anything?"

"Just sitting there," Reba said.

"Okay, well I gave your Mum my word that nothing bad would happen to either of you and she gave me clearance," he held up three tickets. "So, looks like we're going to Hawaii." I was excited. We were going to keep the surveillance going all the way. "Reba," Dad continued. "Here's sixty quid. Go shopping and get us some food for the flight? This is a no-frills airline and it's a five-hour flight." Reba took the money and jumped up, "And get receipts."

#

The airline announced that the flight would be boarding and asked all passengers to line up in groups of A, B, and C. Since the flight wasn't too full, we were in the back half of the B-group. Group A boarded first, and then they announced it was time for family boarding. The Asian couple stood. Mum carried the baby and the clutch bag containing the laptop. Dad folded the stroller, packed it into a sack and they went down the jetway. When the B-group was called, we lined up. Of course, we were going to be the last three people to board. Dad whispered that the airline was going to hold the back rows of the plane open for us.

We boarded and walked down the center aisle. I was the only one with a backpack that looked like luggage, and Reba held a shopping bag stuffed full of sandwiches and snacks. As we made our way down the aisle, I noted that the Asian family had taken the A, B, and C seats of row 7 on the plane. I couldn't see what items the family had stowed or if the clutch bag and laptop were stuffed under the seat in front of one of them. They were occupied playing with the baby and stuffing a bright red dummy in the baby's mouth that got vigorously sucked. They never looked at us or paid any notice as we passed. The back four rows of the plane were empty.

"I get the window," Reba said.

"Fine," Dad replied. "I get the aisle close to the bathroom. I hate flying."

Dad stopped and pointed at the middle seat.

"No way." I turned the opposite direction and sat in the aisle seat across from the row he was in. "And what do you mean you hate flying? You did fine when we came over from the UK."

He looked at me with a smirk, "Drugs. I had plenty of them on board and slept through most of the flight if you remember."

He sat in his seat, and I reached across and pulled the barf-bag out of the seat pocket in front of him, "Good. There's one in your seat pocket and we can certainly get a bigger bag if you need it."

"Sod off."

Reba and I had a bit of a laugh. "I'll help take care of him," Reba said. She pulled a packaged tuna sandwich from her bag and showed it to him.

"Great. You can sod off too," Dad said.

We buckled up in the plane and watched the weather pound against the fuselage as water streaked down the windows.

The pilot welcomed everyone on board and announced that the last few bags were being loaded and we were waiting for one more passenger from a delayed flight. About fifteen minutes passed and the additional passenger boarded the jet. It was Agent Wilson. Dressed in loose-fitting slacks, a hooded sweatshirt, and carrying a small clutch bag just like the one we were following, as she walked to the back of the plane. Her expression soured as she caught sight of Reba and me.

She pointed at the last row. "Slide over kid. I get the aisle." She sat, stuffing her bag under the empty seat in front of her. "You didn't tell me this was a family outing?" She looked at Dad.

"He's got the tech, and she's got excellent cover skills."

She shook her head, "It's your funeral, not mine, if anything goes south."

"I got it covered."

"Don't worry," Reba motioned toward my Dad. "We'll make certain nothing bad happens to him."

Agent Wilson huffed, "So where are they?"

"Row 7," I said showing her the image on my tablet that outlined the aircraft and marked the tracker's position ahead of us with a strong signal.

"You may be of some use yet, JP. Anything else?"

"Some of the communications said the guys from Hong Kong wouldn't pay out the big bucks until the demonstration was completed. Lesta said that it would be done by tomorrow.

After that, they're going to exchange the vials and laptop for about 10 million bucks."

"And you know this, how?"

"Once we're airborne, I'll show you the communications I intercepted from their mail server."

"But we seized all their servers."

I smiled, "Not the backup server that took over when the primary went away."

I thought I saw a smile crease her lips, then vanish. The plane door shut, and we pushed back from the gates. During takeoff, we bounced and bounded through rough air. Dad's knuckles were white as he gripped the armrests as though he might snap them off.

Somewhere well over the Pacific Ocean, almost 90-minutes into the flight, conditions smoothed out. Dad ejected from his seat bolting into one of the aft bathrooms.

"Guess he doesn't fly well," Wilson said. "Okay kid, show me what you got related to tomorrow in Hawaii."

I opened my laptop on the center tray table between us and mounted the encrypted drive where I stored all of the captured evidence. Under a folder that was dated two days prior, I opened the communications from the mail server. She read and browsed several mail files and threads.

"They didn't encrypt any of this?"

"The transport was TLS encrypted, both sending and receiving, but not while stored on the mail server," I said making certain she was the only one who could hear me. "After you've browsed through the messages, I'll show you the attachment that brought us here."

She worked through a dozen more messages and then sat back, "Let's see it, the attachment."

I popped open the Autopsy Communication Viewer that showed all of the account relationships. She watched as I moved my mouse toward the account named, man_1. "This account received a message a few hours before our big Korean friend was to be released from jail," I opened the attachment. It was a gold and red picture of the great Fuzanglong. "Look familiar?"

"Dragon from the front gate of the house?"

"Similar. Now, check this timeline and follow along. A few hours before the messages were sent that contained the images, Anton, I call him Mr. Big, exchanged mail with a server in Hong Kong and email account I'd intercepted before. Clearly from Mr. Big, this message expressed frustration that one of the vials had been lost. Check the response," I pointed to the screen. "Threatens to cut the transaction value in half for Mr. Big's bungling. He can only redeem himself if he delivers the whole laptop from the Redwood Lab and if the demonstration is successful."

"Demonstration? What demonstration?" Agent Wilson opened her PC and began taking notes. She also photographed the Autopsy Communication Viewer displaying the mail message.

I shook my head, "Don't know."

"Go ahead."

"There's a message sent through this server to an anonymous Gorilla mail account that reads like a postcard. It has an attachment that is the JPEG image of the dragon," I showed this message and then clicked on the next line. "Right behind that, is a similar message to man_1, who has an account on this mail server."

She snapped a couple more pictures of my screen.

"I asked myself why the big henchman, AKA man_1, would be sent this picture as an attachment. Well, Reba actually spotted that the byte size of the two attachments were different, but the picture of the dragon was absolutely the same," I opened up a file explorer and showed a directory that contained the two images. "So, each image contained different hidden messages," back to Autopsy and the EXIF data analysis section. "Decoding this first one gives the message: *Du hast morgen um 10 Uhr einen Spa-Termin. Laptop im unverschlossenen Auto lassen.*'"

"A spa appointment at 10 AM. Leave laptop in the unlocked car," Agent Wilson translated. "I know German."

"I did the same action with the photograph sent to man_1. It's in Korean and reads: Get laptop by Saratoga spa from car and drop to place 77. Place 77 is the men's toilet by the ticket counters in San Jose Airport, Terminal B."

"And that brings us here. Let me get this straight, you have a tracker of some kind planted on the laptop?"

I nodded, "Yup. And it's in row 7 on this plane now."

"Do you know where Mr. Big is now?"

"Well, we're heading to Honolulu. If you remember, when Reba was grabbed at the cement plant, Mr. Big made a mention of having to go to the Solaris. Anton is Russian, and the Solaris is a huge yacht owned by a Russian oligarch. Not certain if this is the same. The last position of Solaris was in

Turkey. That said, the pictures have GPS coordinates from the iPhone they were taken on that has them in the middle of the North Pacific. End of the day, the ship had to be big enough to have a jet helicopter land on it."

"Russians and Chinese," Wilson commented.

"Yup. That's what makes this interesting. We don't know what the. . . ," air quotes, "demonstration is."

"But we know this laptop we're following is heading to an exchange somewhere in Hawaii?"

"That's a real good conclusion."

At that moment, Dad jumped up again from his seat and ran to the bathroom just behind our seats. Reba slid over to Dad's aisle seat and showed her phone to Agent Wilson. "I figured you guys were going through stuff. Here are the photos of the woman that put the laptop in the Town Car."

"Impressive. Send me those."

"And," I said. "Reba's the one that planted trackers on the Town Car and laptop."

"Nice job, you two. Someday you both may make decent agents."

Dad returned, and Reba was pushed back into her window seat. I shut down my tablet and connected it to a spare battery in my pack just to give it a bit more juice before we landed. Reba pulled out three tuna fish sandwiches that she'd bought back in San Jose. Dad took one look at the sandwiches and headed back to the toilet. Poor guy. Reba passed two sandwiches over. Agent Wilson politely accepted it.

In between bites, I pulled my tablet back out and opened the tracker app.

"What is that machine?" Wilson asked after taking a few small bites of sandwich. "It doesn't look like a commercial tablet."

"It's not. I built it based on Raspberry Pi OS. It runs my trackers and my drones," I showed her the screen showing the tracker was still in place.

I switched to my laptop and ran a passive scan of the plane's wireless network. There were four laptops reported as clients on the network along with a raft of phones and tablets. I sniffed live traffic using CapLoader and watched as the hosts were identified. One system was connected via VPN to the external IP address at Lesta's house. I showed this to Agent Wilson. Dad was fast asleep, and I waved over to Reba. She carefully stepped over Dad and stood in the aisle next to us.

"Someone's online with the network in Lesta's house. The connection's encrypted and I can't see the contents."

Reba nodded and pulled out her backup mobile phone. She walked all the way up the aisle, heading for the forward lavatory. Walking slowly, she passed row 7 and went all the way to the forward toilet. A moment later she returned, still casual as ever. Just another passenger using the bathroom. Showing us a picture on her phone, she advised that the man in row 7 was online with a different laptop -- not the one we we're tailing. "He's on a chat app. The lady and baby are fast asleep. I tried to get a clear picture but didn't want to be too obvious."

"We're clearly following the correct people, then," Agent Wilson said. "No more walking around, girl. Just sit and let's get there."

The rest of the flight went off without any problems. The air over the Pacific was calm, nary a bump to disturb Dad.

#

On arrival, we exited the plane. It was really hot and humid in the Honolulu airport, and we were way overdressed. Sweat beaded on my forehead and Reba kept flipping her hair off her collar to keep cool. The couple with the kid and stroller with the laptop tracker stood at a baggage carousel. We took up a position at the carousel by one of the doors. At least this part of the airport was air conditioned. A lone Pacific Islander man with broad shoulders and wearing a loose-fitting flowered shirt stepped over to us. He held a taxi and tour board with many pictures of Diamondhead, Waikiki, and North Shore surfers. "Taxi? Tours?" He asked.

Dad shook his head, "We're fine."

"Oh, I'm not too sure about that," we all looked at him as he flashed FBI credentials from beneath the sign so only we could see them. "I'm Agent Makoa Kalani. You can call me Mo."

"Ah," Reba said. "Makoa Kalani. The name means a brave or courageous man with regal qualities."

Wilson's eyebrows raised and I too was surprised at this.

"That's me," Kalani smiled as he pointed to pictures on his sign acting like he's selling a tour. All the while Dad and Agent Wilson briefed him on the case.

"Guys," I interrupted. "There's something different here." I pointed to the screen on my tablet. "Reba's original phone is here?"

"What?" Dad asked. "The one that she lost in the helicopter?"

"Yup. It must still have power."

"That means Mr. Big's helicopter is nearby."

"On the other side of the field to be exact."

At that moment, the couple we'd been following pulled two large roller-bags off the carousel and started toward an exit across from us. The tracker moved with them. Probably still in the baby stroller.

"Mo, are you alone?" Wilson asked.

"Nope, two more outside."

"Good, I'll go with the others, and we'll follow the couple as best we can. Stafford," she turned to Dad, "you take them over to wherever that helicopter is and see what you find. You may need HPD for backup."

Mo talked on a hidden radio and gave a description of Agent Wilson as she left baggage claim. She was gone and out to the curb. A different Hawaiian man waved to her, and they went to a small sedan. For us, we followed Mo outside to where he had a brightly colored tour van parked.

"This isn't conspicuous at all," Dad said squeezing into the back with Reba.

"Around here," Mo replied, "nobody pays any attention to a tour bus."

"Get in the front JP and guide him."

A mile down the road, we came to a gated entry to the private hangars. Mo flashed his credentials to the guard, and we were quickly admitted.

"Last row of hangars to the right," I said.

Parked outside a locked hangar was the helicopter. No one was around as Mo stopped between the hangar and craft. "What now?" he said.

Reba opened the back door and jumped out, "I get my phone."

"Crazy girl," Dad said as she dashed over to the helicopter and tried the pilot-side door. It was locked. Then she grabbed the back door handle. Believe it or not, it opened. She reached in fumbling under the seats until she held up her phone.

"It's almost totally dead," she climbed back into her seat.

"Give it to me," I called. "I have a battery. Let's keep it alive. It may contain more evidence. It's good you have a second phone."

"But it's nice to have mine back, too." She passed it to me, and I connected it to a battery pack in my backpack.

Mo held his hand up silencing us. He acknowledged someone calling him. "Seems the subjects have just arrived in a hotel. . ."

"Off Kalakaua Avenue," I interrupted. "The tracker's signal is strong."

"Nothing more to do here," Mo pulled the van around and back toward the exit. "I've taken pictures of this whirlybird. I'll notify air traffic control that it isn't cleared for flight. And have HPD set up a stakeout."

Mo cleared the gate and drove fast down a side street toward the freeway onramp toward downtown Honolulu. "The family has broken up," he repeated what was in his earbud. "Seems the man and baby stayed in the hotel. The woman has come out and is walking down Kalakaua Avenue."

I checked the tracker. It moved down in a south direction along the avenue. "I've got the signal on the laptop. Tell them not to spook her and stay back," I warned.

"Yes, sir," Mo said then repeated my message.

She kept pausing on her walk at street vendors, a technique to detect tails. For now, the agents stayed well back and let the electronics do the job for them. She moved on as we came to park in an open space just near the Duke Paoa Kahanmoku Statue. The tracker is about 700-yards ahead of us on the other side of the street. "Maybe we should get out, act like tourists?" Mo said.

"Good idea," Dad replied reaching for the back door release.

"Wait!" I shouted. "The tracker's crossing the street and heading this way."

Mo went into his full tour guide mode pointing toward the statue and beachfront. Reba and Dad sat forward as though listening intently to Mo as I continued to report. "She's stopping at the statue."

"I see her," Reba said. "She's on a bench facing the statue." Reba kept an eye on her. "She's getting up and walking westward."

Everyone in the van let out a collective sigh. "The tracker's not moving," I noted.

"It's a dead drop," Mo said. "Everyone, watch that bench and keep down." He relayed the message to the rest of the surveillance team. They all closed in on the position, but we were the closest.

"Look! It's Kai-nam!" Reba exclaimed. "Duck."

Both Reba and I fell to the floor to hide. Dad and Mo kept watch. "Which one's Kai?" Mo asked.

"He's the slender Asian kid about four foot eight, with a purple flat top haircut," Reba said from her prayer position on the van floor.

"Got 'em," Mo said. "He's walking toward the bench where the lady had been seated. Now he's sitting in the same spot with his arms stretched downward."

After five tense minutes that felt like twenty, Mo reported that Kai was up and walking back along the boulevard.

"The tracker is moving with him," I said.

"Who's this Kai-nam kid?" Mo said.

"We'll explain later," I swung the passenger door open. "Out of the car everyone. We follow on foot."

It was devilishly hot outside. The sun glared on the water and sandy beach. A lot of beach-clad people soaked in the rays or played in the gentle waves. We filtered through the crowd following the tracker's signal, keeping a reasonable distance. In two blocks, Kai crossed the street heading toward a resort hotel. By now, we were all soaked with sweat. I signaled that the tracker had entered the hotel. Mo notified the other units to move closer to the hotel and cover as many exits as possible. We followed. The lobby was a grand open-air space. Brightly colored parrots hung on trees. Small stands selling trinkets lined the hotel entry. I had hoped for air conditioning, but the area was cooled only by a breeze.

"There's no sign of him," Dad said looking around.

Checking the details, I saw that the tracker was gaining elevation. It leveled off 60 feet up and began moving above us. "He's upstairs," I said. "Possibly the third floor."

The elevator required a room key to activate it. Mo ran over to a hotel staff member, flashed his credentials and we were off and going up the elevator. As we stepped out of the elevator, I gave a thumbs up signal. We were at the same elevation. The tracker was on this floor. I started local guidance that showed the tracker was ahead, then it all went dead.

The tracker stopped signaling. I broke away from the others and ran down the hall to a stairwell exit. I pointed toward the door. Mo pushed me aside and with his hand on his sidearm pushed into the stairwell. We followed.

There was no one inside, just dust and broken electronic fragments on the floor.

"Kai found the tracker and crushed it on the floor," I pointed to the bits on the ground.

"Great," Dad said. "What now?"

Mo called in his radio to the teams. Everything happened so fast that the teams may not have had time to position. An FBI unit reported that they were watching the exit three floors down and that no one left the building.

"We've lost him and the laptop," I said.

DIAMONDHEAD

Mo ordered the other units to maintain position and gave a detailed description of Kai and his clothing. So far, none of the units reported anything.

"CCTV?" Reba asked. "He must still be in the building somewhere."

Mo instructed a unit in the lobby to go to the hotel's security office and see if cameras caught anything. We followed. In the basement of the hotel, the security office was right near the elevators. "You all, wait here," Mo said as he went inside.

After a few minutes that seemed like an eternity, Mo returned. "We had him leave the stairwell on the second floor. He crossed to another stairwell and came out into an exit near the hotel restaurant kitchen entrance. The next, we had him at the loading dock in the back of the building where he climbed into a white BMW X5 SUV. The camera wasn't that good, and we couldn't make out the registration. That's it."

So, little Kai-nam outsmarted us. He could be anywhere. After all this, it was just so deflating.

"You guys," Mo said. "Get a hotel and, for goodness' sake, get some suitable clothes. We'll take it from here."

We paused in the lobby, and I searched for available hotel rooms. There was a motor inn a few blocks away that had a single room with two beds. Dad passed me his credit card and I booked it.

After a short, hot walk, we checked into the room. It was a business class hotel, a term my Dad always used to describe a dive. It had a comfortable but basic room. Inside, Reba stood in front of the air conditioner and let the cold air blow over her. I set up my laptop and equipment on the desk, deciding to log back into my tap that was in Lesta's home network. Maybe there's some mail or messaging traffic in there that will give us a clue. Mr. Big would need to meet up with the Tong members somewhere to make the exchange. But the question of the demonstration that was mentioned in a prior message really bugged me.

"Anything?" Dad asked.

I checked the network captures. There was nothing except idle traffic on the network. No VPN or remote connections. No sign of mail or chat messages either. "Nothing," I replied.

He nodded. "Look, I'm knackered. I'm going to take a shower and nap. Here's my credit card and a few hundred bucks' cash. You and Reba head out and buy us some clothes. I'll be here. Don't get into anything without calling me first."

Reba took the cash and card from him. I felt a bit uneasy leaving my tech in the hotel room, but there wasn't much else we could do. Mobile in pocket and we were off.

We walked back to one of the shops along the street that sold Hawaiian shirts, swim trunks and kit. It wasn't one of those ticky-tack tourist places, but a nice store. Reba grabbed a couple shirts, 2XL for Dad and medium for me, two three packs of underwear, a blouse for her, and a pair of shorts. The bill came to 178 bucks. Reba tapped Dad's credit card.

"Stafford Palmer?" the clerk read the name from the card and looked at the two of us.

"It's my Dad," I replied.

The clerk shook her head and started pulling the items away.

"I have cash," Reba handed the two hundred in cash to the clerk. Deal done, new stuff bagged, and we headed out the front door.

"That was just too quick," Reba remarked as we walked down the avenue toward our hotel. "It's like Kai knew the tracker was there."

"He might have," I said. "It gives off an RF signal. If he had a detection device, he may have sensed the signal following him."

"He made some real smart moves, leading us up to the third floor and then doubling back."

"And," I added, "he didn't even care about any surveillance cameras. He must have known they were there."

"He also knew about the loading dock, other exits, and how to get around."

"He probably prepared for this situation. I thought it was quite telling that the BMW was conveniently positioned at the hotel's rear loading dock."

Reba stopped and looked at me, "Having discovered the tracker that must've tipped him off that we're onto them."

I thought about this for a moment. She's giving them too much credit. "I don't think it did. The tracker would have shown that someone was capable of following. Kai and Lesta probably don't know we're here. They may believe that it's the FBI that planted the tracker. Remember, the FBI ran a warrant on their house. The FBI would be suspected of the intercept of communications. The only problem now is that Mr. Big and team are probably just using cellular networks to connect and running communications through anonymizers like Gorilla. We won't see anything more."

Reba nodded.

"I'd bet they don't know that we have the helicopter staked out and they don't know that you and I are here as well."

"Good point," she said. "The helicopter cuts off an obvious exit. Now, it's up to us but we don't know what to do next or where to go." She walked a bit further down the street, then stopped pointing to a news rack holding today's Honolulu Star newspaper, "Look!"

Reba yanked the paper from the rack, flashing a headline article from the front page at me.

"Hey, girly," the newsagent shouted. "That'll be three bucks."

Reba stared back at him. "It says two-fifty."

"That was this morning's price. Now it's three bucks or put it back nice and neat."

Reba passed him a fiver, that he returned change in a single and four quarters. "Quarters?" she scoffed. "Really!?"

"Put 'em in a video game, girly."

"Whatever!" she pocketed the money. We moved in front of the next store, out of sight of the newsagent.

"Check this article," she opened the paper and tapped her finger on one of the front-page stories. "There's a Chinese delegation that's going to present an award today for one of the last surviving Flying Tigers and his family at a Veteran's home near Diamondhead. The delegation flew in from China to present a golden dragon to the man for his distinguished service to the Chinese people. Are you thinking what I'm thinking?"

"The demonstration?" I said.

"This explains why the statue of Fuzanglong made the long trip along with the vials."

"Let's get Dad." We ran the rest of the way back to the hotel.

In the room, Stafford was on his side and snoring hard. I tried to wake him, but no response. Reba popped into the bathroom emerging in her light blue blouse and shorts. I slipped on the flowered Hawaiian shirt. Again, we tried to wake Dad. He only snored louder and harder.

"Leave him be," Reba said. She used a pen to circle the article in the newspaper. "He should be able to figure out where we're at."

I packed my tech and slung my backpack then headed downstairs behind her.

"Wait," I pulled her to a stop just at the hotel door. "How do we get there? We don't have enough for an Uber."

"Taxi," she flashed the money she had in her pocket.

Outside, Reba waved for a cab that pulled to the front of the hotel. She told the driver where we wanted to go and asked how much, then turned to me. "I'm short about five bucks."

"I've got nothing, Dad entrusted you with all the money."

She talked again to the driver then went to open the back door of the cab. "He'll run the meter and drive as far as he can toward the Veteran's home and drop us when it hits the amount."

We got dropped three blocks from the Veteran's home. The driver pointed to a large white, two-story building with a dark red tile roof and said that it was our destination.

We were just a block away as we passed a neighborhood park adjacent to the Veteran's home. I pulled Reba into the park. "Let's get an aerial view of this place and what surrounds it." I pulled the grey drone from my bag and my tablet. The battery was fully charged, and, in a flash, I had the four motors extended and ready for flight.

The drone climbed high giving us a full view of the home. The building stood on a corner lot. It was "L" shaped with a main entrance midway down the front of one wing. The structure was modeled in an old, Hawaiian plantation style. Exterior shutters hinged open from the top leaving 6 or so inches for air to circulate in through an open window. An American flag hung over the main entrance.

I marked a flight path for the drone that arced around the building in wider and wider circles allowing the camera to see any activity in a near region of the home. Reba and I watched the screen intently.

Three men stood near the back of a trades van just beyond a block from the home. The rear doors of the van were wide open and there were two ladders on roof. The interesting thing was the white car parked about 10 feet behind the van.

"That's a white BMW SUV, isn't it?" Reba asked.

"Could be," I put a marker on the SUV and had the drone hold position. "I can drop down to probably 60 feet or so without them hearing the drone. There's very little air movement to mask the sound." I ordered the drone down and kept it high enough. I zoomed the camera in.

"I know that one," Reba pointed at the image. "He's the scientist guy from the cement factory." She pulled her original cell phone out and showed the picture of the man she snapped that fateful night in Frisco.

"I think you're right. Can you make out what he's doing?"

"Looks like he's putting something into a long tube thing."

"It's not a tube," I said. "That's the statue of Fuzanglong."

"Dang. They're loading the vial into the gaping mouth of the dragon. That's what they're going to present to the veteran here and then kill everyone in the Veteran's home," she shrieked. "We need to call Agent Wilson, now!" She tapped at her mobile phone.

I could hear the ringing sound through her phone. She waited, tapping her foot impatiently. Wilson didn't answer.

"She's not answering," Reba said. "I left a voicemail. It's up to us." Reba said.

I recalled the drone. Reba ducked out of the park and ran toward the home.

I packed the drone and sent an urgent SOS message to Dad's mobile including the geo-coordinates for our location.

An arm grabbed my shoulder and twisted me around.

"I think I know you," Mr. Big, Anton Andropov, said gripping my shoulder in his meaty huge hand. "You won't be needing this anymore." He grabbed my mobile then wrapped his huge hand around it until the phone popped in half. "Kids play way too much with mobile phones these days."

The hand on my shoulder slid around the back of my neck. His other hand made a huge fist around the remaining bits of my broken phone until they crumbled to the ground.

"Let me go!" I shouted.

"Keep struggling. Please. I'd just love to snap your neck." His voice was soft and very calm.

I went limp and complied.

"Ah, too bad. I haven't snapped a neck in a real long while," he strode off across the lawn that led to the Veteran's home. I walked along but my feet were barely touching the pavement. "My son," he continued, "Lesta, doesn't like it when I hurt malyutkas. Oh. Little things. I usually agree. But you've turned up too many times interfering with my plans. We stepped around a side driveway to the lot at the back of the building by a kitchen entrance and another loading dock. A tall, fit looking man in a sleek black suit met us by the backdoor.

"What's this?" The man said nodding toward me.

"*Shpion*," Anton replied in Russian.

"Do we cancel?"

"No. Push on. We just add one more to the demonstration," Anton said. "This way, sonny." He pulled me through the side door and down a flight of cement stairs and into a basement storage area. He slapped me down on a wooden chair in the center of the room. I tried to stand but he pressed me back down, then waved a single hairy finger in front of my face. "Be good and you won't get too hurt."

The man passed him a role of grey duct tape. Anton lashed my body, arms and hands to the chair. "Any last words, sonny?" Anton flicked a blade open at my face.

"You won't kill me!" I said.

"Me? Kill you? *Nyet*." He stepped back a bit. "Him. I can't guarantee the same." Both men laughed. Anton was dead serious now. He slit a four-inch piece of tape and used the knife to punch a hole in the middle of the slice. Then paste it over my mouth. I had an air hole, but nothing else.

"Do svidaniya, sonny," Anton and the other man left the storage room shutting the door in their wake. I heard them climb the stairs.

The basement was lit by sunlight streaming through three opaque hopper windows. I struggled against my restraints, but my arms and legs were fully restricted. I rocked back and forth in the chair, trying to move it toward the shelves behind me, but then fell over on my side. Now I couldn't move at all.

The door to the basement opened and someone stepped in. I couldn't turn my head up from the floor, but I knew someone was there. There was a shuffling sound and then the sound of someone rummaging through a bag. My drone dropped just a foot from my face to the cement floor. Then a boot crashed through the drone grinding the plastic parts into the floor. "You won't be needing this anytime soon." It wasn't Anton's voice. I struggled to look around but still couldn't see the person's face.

A hand grabbed the side of the chair that held my arms and legs and pulled me upright. It was Lesta, Anton's son. He grinned at me. "You won't be needing this either," he held my tablet PC between his two fingers and motioned as though to drop it next to the drone bits. "Now, what say you tell me where your little girlfriend is?"

I groaned and squeaked as best I could through the duct tape gag.

"What was that? I can't understand you." He dropped the tablet from face height to the floor. It landed with a thud.

I tried to speak again but only grunts and groans came from the mask as he held his boot just above the tablet. Then, he relaxed and stepped a bit closer. His fingers peeled the edges of the duct tape from my mouth and then ripped it off like a nurse removing a bandage. It stung. I groaned again. "I don't know where she is," I blurted.

"So, she is here."

I said nothing.

"It doesn't really matter anyway."

"This is madness, you're going to kill innocent people with that gas when it's released."

Lesta looked a bit shocked, then leant his face real close to my ear. "You might be one of those innocent people real soon, too. Because you don't have one of these." He dangled a gas mask in front of my face.

"Why?"

"You know, it really doesn't matter where your girlfriend is. If she's upstairs, she'll have an experience her family will never forget."

"I thought you were the one that wouldn't hurt kids."

"Sorry." He straightened and kicked a few of the bits of my drone around. "Now, my father's in control of all this."

"But why?"

"Oh, wow. You really, really want to know?" He spoke next in a falsetto voice, mimicking a child's voice, "No, save me, I'm too young to die?" Then back to normal. "Instead, you want to know why we're doing this before you go out forever."

He kicked my tablet PC across the room and lobbed my backpack over with it. "Okay, I'll tell you. After all, every good villain tells the condemned man the secret. It's like this. The Tong want a demonstration for a lot of people about the capability of this new toxin. And, what a better way than having a 97-year-old member of the Flying Tigers in residence to receive a toxic gift from the glorious People's Republic of China."

I shook my head.

"What? You don't get it, do you?" he leant forward resting both of his arms on my arms that were still lashed to the chair. "You don't track world politics. You see, the People's Republic of China promised universal suffrage to the people of Hong Kong but backed out. There will be witnesses here that will blame the PRC. Back in Hong Kong, another demonstration will be held. For this, the PRC gets the blame, and the people of Canton may get some small amount of justice through an enhanced relationship with the West."

"That's actually kind of brilliant. But how do you accomplish this?"

Lesta smiled and slipped off his glasses, ready to put on the mask. "We've swapped the dragons. Anytime now, the real Chinese delegation will present our dragon as a gift. A final gift. From my perspective, any heat applied to China is heat not applied to us."

"Russia?" I asked.

Lesta grinned, "Hardly. Mother Russia is an ally of China now. They know nothing of this."

Lesta checked the restraints binding me and tapped my cheek. "All nice and snug. Sweet dreams, kid." He waved the mask again and moved toward the door as a piercing alarm sounded in the building. The sound echoed through the halls and into the basement. "What the heck?" Lesta shouted as he dashed out.

I struggled against the restraints and fell over again onto my side. This time I kicked and thrashed as hard as I could trying to move the chair along the floor. This is it. I can't get out. This must be how my short life will end lashed to a chair and gassed out of my mind. I paused for a second. The alarms piercing chirps continue and my ears are ringing with the echo in the storeroom.

A few moments later, Reba kicked the door open and dashed in. She held her cell phone. She ran across the room, feet crunching on the parts of my drone scattered everywhere. "Reba!" I shouted.

She pulled at the tape trying to unwrap my bindings. Dad appeared behind her and stomped on the legs of the chair breaking the wooden legs and back. He lifted me up and carried me as we all climbed out of the basement to the fresh air outside.

Fire trucks and police units were everywhere. I could see what looked like the Chinese delegation off to one side standing with Agent Mo. Agent Wilson and two fire crew came up to me and began cutting my arms and legs free of the chair's remains. I looked up at the Veteran's home as green smoke billowed from one of the upstairs windows. They set me on the rear fender of an ambulance.

"What happened?"

Reba stood holding her hands on her knees breathing deeply. "Thank goodness my phone had access to your location," she said.

I noticed a bit of blood smeared on her lips and a puffy cheek.

"Seems like you two got into the thick of it again," Dad said. "But Reba here did a great job. She went in and intercepted the dragon just as the device in its mouth was about to go off."

"Your girlfriend took on one of the Tong members as we were pulling up then yanked a fire alarm." Agent Wilson added. "Are you okay?"

I nodded, "Just bruised. Did you catch them?"

Wilson looked over to Dad. An exchange of glances that told me no. "We got one of the Tong members. No Lesta, Mr. Big or Kai."

"The BMW," I said. "If I had my equipment, we'd have pictures of it."

"Reba told us, and we have the vehicle."

Mo ran over at that moment. "The stakeout is in place at the chopper. Seems the pilots are getting the bird ready for flight. I've told them to wait until any passengers arrive." He returned to his van and stood by the open door.

"You have to catch Anton and Lesta," I said while a paramedic wrapped a blood pressure cuff around my arm and clipped an oximeter to my finger. I tried to stand, but Dad flicked his finger on my forehead and pushed me back down.

Every resident of the Veteran's home was successfully evacuated, and a hazmat crew made final preparations to enter the building.

Agent Mo Kalani trotted back again. "We got 'em," he said to Agent Wilson. "Lesta and Kai showed up at the helicopter and HPD swept them up along with the pilots. The chopper's impounded as well."

"What about Mr. Big, Anton Andropov?" I said.

He shook his head. "No sign of him. But someone of his stature shouldn't be too hard to locate on this island. I've put out an Island-wide BOLO for him."

"Nice job all of you," Agent Wilson said as she walked past Dad. "Hope you have a quiet flight home."

EPILOG: JUST ANOTHER DAY

And that's the end of my first journal. At least the parts that I documented and can remember. Reba played a special role in this case and several subsequent cases, right up to her extracting me from Bulgaria. My right shoulder ached as I stood and walked ankle deep in the warm Caribbean Sea. How would I repay her now.

Back when we were teens, I recalled us flying home to a warm reception at the airport. We were transferred in large limousines to our homes where Agents Thompson waited with all our families. Wilson and Thompson labeled both Reba and me as heroes.

Mama Ng and my Mum were in tears as the agents presented us with FBI citations of honor that were actually signed by the President of the United States.

Reba and I never returned to Leigh High School that year or any other public school in San Jose. We were given full scholarships to attend Pinegrove Alpha Academy and expected to board on site at the campus. I remember Agent Wilson saying that they could better keep an eye on us both if we were in a private boarding school.

But my fondest memory was the long, deep kiss I received from Reba once we were alone. That made everything worth it.

At the new school, Reba quickly integrated into the soccer team, and I joined the cybersecurity club. We saw our families on weekends and during school events. I missed having my Dad around every day and getting sage lessons from my Mum. But it was okay. Occasionally, Agent Wilson would show up bringing some little piece of evidence for me to tinker with.

I reclined alone on my lounger with my feet coated in warm white Caribbean sand. Reba was the only thing on my mind. I thought about everything that happened at the end of our sophomore school year while in a protected private academy where we just so happened to break up a human trafficking ring, but that's in my next journal that I just might fish out from the attic.

Once we graduated, Reba got sponsored by the FBI special operations branch and went on to The Citadel outside Charleston, South Carolina. I was given a full ride scholarship to Carnegie Melon University to study computer science and forensics. I received an assignment to the National Security Agency. Over the years, our paths crossed until she stopped coming home for holiday dinners. I lost touch with her, until I followed signal intelligence related to a Chinese satellite that led me to Bulgaria. I so wanted to activate my systems to see if I could find her but that would violate my boss's orders to stay offline, and they would surely see me.

END: UNTIL RESCUING THE LOST

Jason Palmer's Tips to Stay Safe Online:

PRIVACY TIPS...

"Keep your personal info private"
You shouldn't share your full name, address, phone number, school name, or passwords with anyone online, except your parents or trusted adults.

"Be careful what you post"
Once something is online, it can be hard or even impossible to take down. Please think before you post pictures or videos.

"Know your privacy settings"
Talk to a trusted adult about understanding and using the privacy settings on the apps and websites.

"Strong passwords are key"
Use a mix of uppercase and lowercase letters, numbers, and symbols. Don't share your passwords with anyone. Not even your best friends.

Dear Reader,

They thought they could use the internet to exploit the vulnerable. They clearly haven't met me.

The Digital Detective returns to face the horrors of human trafficking in book two, **Rescuing the Lost.**

My antivirus is up to date, but my patience is running low. Book 2 is coming soon!

Happy reading,

CLOUD10® STUDIOS

ESCAPE INTO A WINTER WONDERLAND
with Christmasaur™ and friends.

With a parent's help, visit www.christmasaur.com to learn more